WITCH AT LAST

A JINX HAMILTON MYSTERY - BOOK 3

JULIETTE HARPER

*"I am not afraid of storms
for I am learning how to sail my ship."*

— Louisa May Alcott

ACKNOWLEDGMENTS

First to the readers, who have believed in Jinx from the beginning. There is no magic without you. Special thanks to our beta readers, Brenda Trimble, Larry Trimble, and to our faithful and patient proofreader, Sandra Jackson. To Delia Ruth Williamson for the ongoing fairy dust. And to Jennifer Radcliff, for her paging and design work and for being our first and constant friend in the self-publishing world.

1

"What did you do over the summer, Jinx?"

Oh, you know, the usual. Found out I was a witch, talked to some dead folks, caught a serial killer, released an immortal sorceress and then had to figure out how to put her back. Nothing exciting.

That summer when all those things happened? I would have given almost anything for a good healthy case of *boredom*. Or even just a return to the normal summer days of my childhood. Back when I spent hours putting fireflies in Mason jars, digging worms to go fishing at the creek, or reading books up in the tree house I shared with my BFF, Tori.

When I had to write those "what I did during summer break" essays on the first day of school, I tried *not* to describe our actual family vacations in detail. Short version: Dad is a Type A driver with a good vocabulary.

That same editorial caution applies to the events of the summer before my 30th birthday. Depending on my audience, the truth might land me in the psych ward. I'm counting on you all to be a little more open-minded.

That was the summer when everything changed.

At first the revelations were more or less personal. The news that you're a witch with real powers carries plenty of life altering bang for the buck. Foolishly, I thought I might be able to keep that behind closed doors. Yeah, not so much.

When September rolled around, I really did head back to school, but not in a way the PTA would ever support. I don't want to get ahead of myself though. We have a lot of ground to cover. For now, let's just say that by summer's end, I found out the *whole* world was different than I had ever imagined. Let me give you a few highlights so we're all on the same page.

Aunt Fiona died in the spring. She left me her store in Briar Hollow, North Carolina, a sleepy little burg off the Blue Ridge Parkway. I quit my job waiting tables at Tom's Cafe, loaded up my four cats, and moved into the apartment over the shop.

That first night, half awake and feeling sentimental about my aunt, I muttered something about wanting her magic. People had believed my kind, eccentric aunt was a "witch woman," but I was thinking more along the lines of fairy godmother.

(We'll get to the real fairies before we're done. Just be patient.)

Maybe there was no pumpkin coach pulled by four white mice, but Aunt Fiona did leave me everything she owned. The inheritance elevated me from being a minimum-wage-plus-tips waitress to owning a small business.

My head reeled with gratitude, as it should have, but when I said that little bit about wanting her magic, I didn't realize it was a complete "be careful what you ask for" moment.

Trust me on this. Do *NOT* go rubbing a lamp if you're not ready to deal with a genie.

The next morning my four cats woke me up demanding breakfast. I wasn't fast enough, so they resorted to coercion. Winston jumped up on the dresser and sent a figurine crashing to the floor -- or at least he tried.

I caught the fragile object -- with my mind. Yep. I levitated that little porcelain duck right back up on the dresser while the cats watched with studied disinterest.

At the time, I told myself that I really wasn't awake and it was all just my imagination. Until I walked into the kitchen and had a conversation with my dead aunt's ghost. My unthinking request from the night before had been granted. I was a witch, with no way to refuse membership in a club I wasn't anxious to join.

I have since discovered that there are two kinds of witches in this world, and I don't mean the "good witch vs. bad witch" question. When we consider *that* part of the math, the equation gets more difficult, but we're not ready for abracadabra algebra just yet. Let's just stick with the basics.

First, we have folks who practice a religion called Wicca. They self-identify as witches for spiritual purposes. Their worldview centers on principles like taking personal responsibility for your actions, living as you like so long as it harms no one, and healing the planet. (Also, it looks like the casseroles at the Solstice potluck are pretty fantastic. Who knew you could do that with tofu?)

Then there are people like me. We're hereditary witches. Magic is in our genes. It's not so much something we create, as a force we access from the world around us. Sometimes even ordinary people can tap into that force by accident if they're scared enough or so focused on an outcome nothing will get in their way. You know those stories you read about mothers lifting cars off their kids after an accident? Those incidents always get written off to adrenaline, but that's the easy, pat answer.

Let me give you another example. Say your Uncle Willie is a big Tarheels football fan and he's convinced the team won the opening game of the season because he was wearing a particular pair of socks. For the rest of the season, he won't let Aunt Maud wash those socks no matter how much they stink. Do the socks actually help the team win?

Most of the time, no, but if the Tarheels haven't won in ten seasons and then someone finds Uncle Willie's magic socks, wears them to a game, and the Tarheels decimate the competition? Then you might have an object on your hand that's been imprinted with magic.

Ninety-nine percent of all good luck charms out there have no actual power, I'm just saying don't rule out the one percent. You'll see why by the end of my story.

So, back to hereditary witches.

We do have one thing in common with the Wiccans, however, which is a belief in The Rule of Three. The concept is simple. Whatever energy you put out in the world comes back to you three times. Karma to the third power.

Sure enough, before that summer ended, I experienced *three* major events that moved me toward real acceptance of my status as a brand new witch -- setting myself up for the next batch of *three*, but of course I had no way of knowing that then.

If I had? I might have booked it out of there *triple* quick.

In the immediate aftermath of finding out that I'm a witch, Tori and I nabbed us a serial killer. That was major experience number one. It was my first opportunity to see that the powers I was resisting could be used to help other people, and it broadened my understanding of the power all living beings have to communicate with one another.

Dealing with a stone-cold insane killer was not on my bucket list, but I did come away with some new friends. Granted, they're all dead, but that condition is not as self-limiting as I once imagined.

The really important takeaway from the experience was being able to give the spirits of two murdered women a measure of peace. No matter what else I might have been feeling at the time, helping them was a positive and humbling accomplishment that made me more open to seeing my powers as a potential good thing.

If I'd stuck with the humble part alone, all would have been well. Instead, I got a swelled head and tried to do something I was in no way qualified to do. That put us in the position of dealing with a resurrected sorceress with a really big chip on her shoulder.

Cut to Jinx's Really Big Summer Adventure, Scene Two. Throwing water on the Wicked Witch.

Okay. Not really.

We zapped her with blue lightning, but the effect was similar -- or so we thought.

A number of things happened along the road to major event number two, including my acquisition of a 2' tall "minion" named Darby. He's officially a brownie, who has become the chief barista of our new espresso bar. He blends the beans, calibrates the grinds, and maintains the place at a level that makes Mr. Clean look like a slacker.

All the while staying discreetly invisible.

Literally.

Invisible.

It's a cool trick I wouldn't mind mastering, but that one doesn't seem to be in my witchy skill set.

Oh. The espresso bar. I almost forgot. Let's go ahead and cover that one.

Tori is in business with me now. We've wanted to be entrepreneurs since we were kids running our first lemonade stand. Aunt Fiona's generosity has made that dream a reality as well.

Without Fiona's personality, the store lacked focus. Not that I would necessarily call Fiona a paragon of concentration, but she was really the reason people came through the front door. While her approach to inventory might have been haphazard, Fiona knew how to help people with a gentle word, a cup of herbal tea, or a crystal to wear to soothe their worried minds.

I can almost hear you asking, "So was she just being a kind old lady, or was she working magic?"

Here's a little insight for you.

Kindness is a form of magic.

Inheriting the store was the easy part. Making it my own was harder.

When I was at a loss about how best to proceed, Tori came up with the idea for an espresso bar. She put up half the money for the equipment and renovations, which included adding a micro apartment behind the store where she now lives.

It's good having Tori here, especially after the whole Wicked Witch thing.

We can get back to that now.

The Wicked Witch, also known as Brenna Sinclair was a gift that just kept on giving.

In trying to get rid of her, we found out that Brenna is Tori's great-great-great-something grandmother.

Which is kinda okay, because I'm the great-great-something granddaughter of a Cherokee witch ... who was also Tori's great-great-something-grandmother.

Which makes me and Tori related.

But only in the South where genealogy has been raised to a sacred art form.

Confused about the exact nature of the relationship? Good. So are we, which is why we stick to the all-purpose term "cousin."

Obviously we didn't figure out all those details by ourselves. Myrtle helped.

Who is Myrtle?

Well, the better question might be "what" is Myrtle.

She's my store.

Or potentially a fairy queen.

Or currently the older woman who oversees the hidden lair in my basement.

Actually, she's all of the above. And, yes, there is a lair.

Let me explain. We were about to learn more about Myrtle's true nature and her origins, which made all those disjointed pieces fall into place. Going in, however, we were pretty much operating on the same level of information you now have.

So what were the lessons of major event number two? Knowing who your "people" are really does matter in life, everybody needs a little help from their friends, and when someone you love is in danger, you find the courage to face the wicked witch.

That pretty much catches you up to the eve of the third big event, which is where we're starting.

Two things happened that day.

First, I opened the front door of the store early that morning to get the Sunday paper and found a little white box waiting for me on the doorstep.

When I opened it, I found a coffee cup with a picture of the Wicked Witch of the West astride her broom from *The Wizard of Oz*. The caption read, "Fire burn and cauldron bubble, this witch needs coffee or there'll be trouble." The nestled letter card in the box read, "Good luck on your new espresso bar. - A satisfied customer."

When I showed the cup to Tori, she laughed and said, "We should start an in-house collection of funny cups. I'll put this one up on the shelf behind the counter."

Lowering my voice, I said, "Don't you think it's a little creepy that the 'satisfied customer' chose a cup with a witch on it?"

"Come on, Jinksy," she laughed, "it's just a coincidence. Not everything is some big conspiracy."

Let me commend to you the immortal words of Joseph

Heller from *Catch-22*. "Just because you're paranoid doesn't mean they aren't after you."

Right on the heels of finding the cup, I worked up the nerve to put in a phone call to my mother, Kelly. Her BFF is Tori's mom, Gemma.

With everything else I'd learned from the day I inherited the store right up to that morning, the one thing that hit me like a 2x4 was discovering that my good Southern Baptist mother had known about the family magic all along and kept the truth from me on purpose.

What the *heck* was she *thinking*?

It's one thing to not tell me when a guy she didn't like called to ask me out, but I could have used a few years of junior witch league before getting tossed in the middle of a metaphysical sorority formal with no idea which wand to use at supper.

That Sunday when I picked up the phone and called Mom, I was already annoyed before she even answered. For the record, Mom wasn't thrilled when I moved to Briar Hollow, giving up my job of 11 years to run "Crazy Aunt Fiona's" store.

"Norma Jean!" Mom exclaimed cheerfully. "How are you, Sugar?"

Wincing at the unwelcome use of my Southern double name, I said, "We need to talk."

An ominous silence filled the next few seconds, and then Mom, drama queen that she is, said, "Is it cancer?"

"*What*?!" I spluttered. "No! For God's sake, Mom!"

A hurricane-force sigh of relief blasted through the receiver. "Oh, thank God. Do *not* scare me like that!"

"How can I scare you when you haven't even let me say anything yet?" I asked crossly.

"Well, fine," Mom huffed in return. "What is it?"

Steeling myself for what I assumed would be vehement denial, I seized the proverbial bull by the horns, and waded in.

"I know the truth about our family's magic," I said. "I know about Knasgowa and Alexander Skea. I know about Brenna Sinclair. And I know that *you* know, so don't you dare lie to me anymore."

Sorry to keep backtracking on you, but we really do need to pause for station identification.

Alexander Skea was a Scotsman who came to America in 1786, just a few steps ahead of his great-grandmother, Brenna Sinclair, an immortal sorceress who had recently escaped from 108 years of imprisonment in a cave on the Orkney Islands.

Brenna gained her magic by cutting a deal with a dark power. She gave up her ability to have children along with her humanity. When she became pregnant by Hamish Crawford in 1679, Brenna was more than a little surprised.

She did, however, see the pregnancy as an incredible opportunity to establish her own line of hereditary witches and, I assume, engage in some evil plot to take over the world because that's pretty much what evil sorceresses do.

By the time I heard the story about Brenna and her baby daddy, Hamish, a couple of centuries had obscured many of the details and I wasn't ready to sit down and clear up the specifics with Brenna herself. Which I could have done, since I'd just released her from her second imprisonment in a grave right smack in the middle of the Briar Hollow cemetery.

How the heck did I manage that? Good question.

Back in 1697, Hamish, and a local Druid, Duncan Skea, trapped Brenna in the cave so Hamish could escape, leaving Duncan to raise the child, Alastair, as his own.

In time, Alastair fathered Angus, who was Alexander's dad. When Brenna escaped, Angus sent his son to America with Darby (my new brownie minion) as his personal servant. Alexander intended to pull a disappearing act, but he met and fell in love with a Cherokee woman, Knasgowa, who was herself a witch. She protected him from Brenna until 1853. Then, dying of cancer, Knasgowa managed to imprison Brenna again -- in Knasgowa's own grave.

Enter Genius Girl, a.k.a. "me."

The plan was to free my ghostly friends who were, for some reason, trapped inside the walls of the local cemetery. In trying to do that, I turned Brenna loose. And I also raised the spirits of all the people in the graveyard I *didn't* know. The ones who were usually peacefully dead, not enjoying an active afterlife.

Thankfully, they're all back where they belong now, with the exception of former Briar Hollow Mayor, Howard McAlpin, who has assumed a new office. He's the ghost in residence at the courthouse directly across the street from my shop.

With all those ghosts wandering around town and becoming frustrated enough to manifest in the real world, Briar Hollow has picked up a reputation as a paranormal tourist destination.

My best dead friend from the cemetery, Confederate Colonel Beauregard T. Longworth, has taken it upon himself to keep the resulting economic boost going. Two or three times a week he briefly materializes at the base of the Confederate monument.

Beau has turned out to be quite the actor. He strikes a melancholy military pose, gazing sadly up at the gray granite soldier erected to commemorate the deaths of local boys in what Beau refers to as the "Late Unpleasantness."

The ghost hunters who snap Beau's picture don't know his sadness is real. He was a cavalry colonel whose men were killed a few miles outside of town when Beau failed to order proper reconnaissance of the area. He blames himself for their deaths, which is why he still walks the earth.

The one benefit of having raised all the cemetery ghosts is that I did manage to free my spirit friends from their entrapment inside the graveyard walls. I had expected the ghosts to move on to whatever is "next," but they're all still here, including a spectral coonhound named Duke.

Putting the other ghosts back in their plots involved some benign grave robbing and even a close encounter of the mountain lion kind, but once things calmed down and returned to normal -- that being a setting on the dryer -- I was determined to just enjoy the rest of the summer.

That meant making a success of the espresso bar (which the locals, to Tori's annoyance, persist in calling a "coffee shop,") and spending quality time with my handsome next-door neighbor / boyfriend, Chase McGregor.

Unfortunately, all the unanswered questions about our heritage wouldn't leave Tori or me alone, so we decided we had no other choice but to confront our mothers.

Ever see a game show called *Let's Make a Deal?* That phone call to my mom opened the infamous Door #3.

For the game show uninitiated, Door #3 almost never reveals the cool stuff. Unlucky contestants who pick Door #3 typically walked off with a lifetime supply of chicken noodle soup, while the guy who goes with Door #2 kicks back in his brand new convertible.

You're not going to believe what was behind my Door #3.

2

The day we spoke on the phone, mom surprised me. She immediately said Tori and I should come over to neighboring Cotterville to discuss what we'd learned.

"I'll call Gemma," Mom said. "We'll all sit down and talk."

"Gemma knows about you?" I asked.

"Of course she does," Mom said, "she's my best friend."

I couldn't help myself. I had to ask. "So, are you *both* witches?"

There was a long pause. So long I almost asked if she was still there. Then Mom cleared her throat and said simply, "Yes, we are, but we don't do that kind of thing anymore."

Before I could ask anything else, the line went dead.

When I told Tori about the conversation, her eyes grew wide. "You are not *serious!*" she said incredulously. "They've been conspiring all these years?"

I could not believe *that* was where her mind went first. "You're most focused on a potential conspiracy than on finding out that your mother is a witch?" I asked incredulously.

Since the two of us have been guilty of our own fair share of "conspiring" to keep things from the moms, it really didn't seem like we could cast too many stones in that department.

"The witch thing doesn't surprise me on all kinds of levels," Tori grinned. "The fact that they managed to keep their mouths shut all these years *astounds* me."

Okay that I would give her. The moms vehemently denied any participation in "gossip," preferring to style themselves as "informed." Working within their definition, let's just say they believed strongly in the power of information sharing.

By the end of that day, we learned how much we'd underestimated our mothers. It happens at some point in every daughter's life -- that moment when you realize the woman who raised you isn't stupid. You start reviewing every lie and half-truth you ever told. How much did she know? *All* of it.

It's hard to say what Tori and I were expecting when we sat down with Kelly and Gemma in Mom's disturbingly Laura Ashley-designed front living room. However, the fact that we were *in* that room, told us they meant business.

Mom doesn't have plastic covers on all the furniture, but there are strict rules about when that room gets used; major holidays, wakes, and when the preacher comes to call. For a normal visit, we should have been sitting around the kitchen table drinking sweet tea.

"Where's Dad?" I asked, as we all claimed our places. By habit, I brushed off the seat of my jeans before perching gingerly on one of the chairs.

"Where do you think he is?" Mom asked. "Fishing. He and the boys are spending the weekend at the river. He won't be home until late tonight."

"Does he know . . ." I started.

"No," she said with quiet authority, "he does not, and we're going to keep it that way, young lady."

I recognized a direct order when I heard one, and replied with a contrite, "Yes, ma'am."

After a minute or two, Mom cleared her throat and said, "You want to ask some questions. Well, here we are. Ask."

Before either of us could speak, Gemma issued a warning.

"Just so you know," she said, "there's not going to be any ganging up on Kelly here today."

Gemma is the taller of the two women, standing an inch or so under six feet. My Mom is petite and tiny, straining to make five feet on her best day. In fact, the moms are a study in contrasts in all kinds of ways, not just height. Tori gets her blond hair and fearless personality from Gemma. Mom and I have darker hair and are more cautious by nature. And like the daughters they raised, the BFF moms are protective of one another. Whatever we were about to discuss, Gemma was on high alert to see to it Mom didn't get hurt.

I cut my eyes over at Tori who flashed me a "danger, Will Robinson" look. We'd heard that tone in Gemma's voice before. She is far more formidable than my mom, *and* she'd just given up cigarettes. Let's just say the effect on her disposition was . . . less than positive.

"Nobody wants to gang up on anybody," I said carefully. "It's just that we know everything now and we want to hear your side of the story."

Gemma snorted. "Everything?" she said derisively. "Little girl, you don't know half of *anything*, much less *all* of everything."

Feeling like I was tip-toeing through a maternal minefield, I said, "Okay. Tell us what we don't know."

To my horror, Mom's eyes instantly filled with tears.

The best way I can describe my mother is "self-contained." She's always been a little high-strung, but in a *together* sort of way, like one of those hens you expect will go flapping off at any second but never does. Other than daubing her eyes at funerals, I'd never seen Mom cry. And it unnerved me.

Mom looked at Gemma and said, tremulously, "I can't."

Gemma was sitting on one end of the sofa and Mom was to her immediate left in a big floral wingback that made her diminutive frame look even smaller. Gemma reached over and took hold of her hand. "You don't have to," she said. "I'll do it."

I saw Mom squeeze Gemma's fingers, but she didn't say anything. She just nodded a couple of times and reached for a tissue from the box on the end table.

"We were freshmen in high school," Gemma began, drawing in a deep breath like she was steeling herself to do something tremendously hard. "We wanted to be cheerleaders, but we weren't popular enough. We . . . we cast a spell."

When she didn't go on, Tori asked the obvious question. "A spell to do what, Mom?"

My mother was the one who answered, her voice breaking on the words. "We weren't trying to hurt them," she said.

"Kell," Gemma said gently, "we don't know that we *did* hurt them."

With tears now rolling down her face, Mom said, "They died, didn't they?"

Died?

Whoa.

Not where I had seen this conversation going.

"Who died?" I asked.

"The two most popular girls on the cheerleading squad," Gemma answered. "We cast a spell to keep them from coming to school the day of the tryouts. They were best friends, like your Mom and me. Sally Beth picked Jo Anne up on their way into town. Their families lived up in the mountains. It was raining that morning, and the car ran off the road. Both girls were killed in the crash."

A heavy silence settled over the room, broken only by my mom's soft sniffles. Gemma was still holding Mom's hand. I went over to her, but Mom wouldn't look at me, so I sat down on the floor in front of her chair.

When her eyes finally met mine, I said, "It might not have been the spell."

"Maybe," she replied, sadness filling her features, "but we'll never know for sure, will we?"

"So that's why you never told me the truth about our family?" I prodded.

"Of course it is!" Mom cried with sudden ferocity. "No good *ever* comes of magic."

Which wasn't true, but I could understand why she felt that way.

Maybe what came out of my mouth next should have remained unsaid. Maybe I could have waited for another day, but I didn't. Looking back, it was just as well. Frustration flooded through me. I had to live my own life and make my own choices, which I couldn't do if people kept withholding vital information I needed.

So far, my own magic hadn't hurt anyone. But a few weeks before, in another moment of frustration, when I was tired and scared, I started to lose my temper. With no warning, objects in the room levitated and the temperature went up a few degrees.

Coming into my powers with no warning threw me into a rollercoaster of emotional reactions. First I went from denial to curious exploration and then idiotic over-confidence. But none of it scared me as much as the idea that if I didn't learn to control my powers, they could be dangerous.

Why does the wording on the inside of a fan belt suggest it be installed with the engine off? Because some moron tried it with the engine on and it didn't work out well.

Using witchcraft without training is pretty much the same thing.

I'm good with zapping evil sorceresses with blue lightning, but not with accidentally frying someone I love.

"Mom," I whispered, trying not to make the words sound like an accusation, "that wasn't your choice to make."

Gemma instantly reared up like a cat about to make history of a rat.

"That'll be enough out of you, Norma Jean," she snapped. "It's not your place to judge. You have no idea what your mama has been through."

At that moment it would have been nice to be a rat because I could have found a deep, dark hole to dive in. Instead, I had to face Gemma's furious glare. Growing up, she was the one Tori and I never wanted mad at us.

When I didn't look away, I saw a flicker of respect move through Gemma's dark eyes, a kind of unspoken "atta girl." She wanted me to stand up to her.

I said very calmly, "Then explain it to me. Help me understand."

Gemma started to answer, but Mom stopped her.

"I need to tell the girls," she said simply. Swiveling toward me and Tori, she went on hesitantly, "I . . . I had a kind of . . . well, breakdown after . . . what happened . . . after the . . . accident. When I started to get better, I turned my back on my call . . . on the magical world."

In retrospect, I should have picked up on her hasty self-correction, but it went right over my head.

I knew Tori was just as annoyed as I was over the maternal conspiracy of silence, but she waded in cautiously, "What about you, Mom?" she asked. "Why did you stop using your magic?"

"Kelly didn't ask me to do it," Gemma replied, "I just did it because she needed my support. You don't keep on drinking in front of an alcoholic, and that's just how hard it was on Kelly to accept what happened and renounce her powers."

I'm not sure I would have asked the next question, but Tori and her mom have a different kind of relationship. They're both straight shooters.

"Do you think the spell killed those girls?" Tori asked.

"No," Gemma replied. "We weren't powerful enough to do that, but Kelly believes it did, so I stood by her."

Mom looked at Gemma with a mixture of love and gratitude. "I never would have been able to move beyond it and have a life if it hadn't been for Gemma," she said, "but it was *my* choice for you girls to never know. Surely you can understand why."

Tori broke the awkward silence that followed. "Yes," she said, "but didn't you think that there might come a day when we would *need* to know?"

Mom sighed. "No, Honey" she said, "I didn't. Fiona did, but I thought she was . . ."

"Crazy," I finished. "This is why you had such a fit when I told you I was going to move into the shop. You knew I'd find out about everything."

"Yes," Mom nodded. "I knew Myrtle would ultimately tell you."

My jaw dropped. "You *know* about Myrtle, too?"

"Of course we do," Gemma said. "She's taught generations of witches in both of our families. I'll never forget when she got so irritated with me she winged an arrow right by my nose."

"She did that to you, too?" I asked.

Gemma nodded. "Sure got my attention."

Since Myrtle had used the same . . . instructional technique . . . on me when I was being particularly dense, there was no question the moms knew what they were talking about.

This was the best chance I'd had yet to get an explanation about the spirit animating my shop.

"What *is* Myrtle?" I asked.

"She is aos sí," Mom answered.

I learned the spelling after the fact. What we heard her say that day sounded like, "ace she." The words are Gaelic, a language with letter combinations that defy all explanation.

"What's an aos sí?" Tori asked.

Mom shook her head. "That's for Myrtle to explain," she said. "In fact, Myrtle should tell you the rest. It's just been too long since I've thought about any of this. And Gemma's right. We were never very powerful. Fiona was the one with the talent."

Okay. Wait. Hold on. Myrtle should tell me the *rest*?

I started to press for more details, but Mom's tired face changed my mind.

"Aunt Fiona said I may be the most powerful witch in our family in generations," I said instead. "Did you know that?"

The stricken look on Mom's face seemed completely out of proportion to the question, even considering the story she and Gemma had just told us.

"I was *afraid* of it," Mom answered. "I *am* afraid of what it will mean for you."

"Maybe you should have been afraid of what *not* knowing could mean for me," I muttered without thinking.

Yes, I was too old for a surly teenager moment like that, and I'm not proud of it.

The instant the words were out of my mouth, I regretted them. Gemma drew herself up again to take my head off. I wouldn't have blamed her one bit. But Mom stopped her with a gesture of her hand.

"You're right," Mom said simply. "That's exactly what I should have thought, but I didn't. That's why I have something for you."

She got up and went to the back of the house, returning with a beat-up leather satchel that was just *cool*. The thing fairly screamed, "I have seen the world."

"This belonged to my mother and to Gemma's mother," Mom said, "and their mothers before them, and all the way back through the generations to Awenasa."

"What's in it?" I asked, intrigued and already dying to get my hands on the contents.

"Journals, letters, notes," Mom said. "Everything they thought was important to keep to document their lives as witches."

Tori frowned. "But aren't their grimoires in the basement under the store?" she asked.

Gemma gave her a slightly approving smile. "You're learning fast," she said. "Our side of the family is the scholars, Tori. That's your part in all of this. And, yes, the grimoires are in the basement. These are their personal notes."

Tori frowned. "Wait a minute," she said. "We're descendants of Alexander and Knasgowa's son, Duncan, and Jinx is descended from Knasgowa's daughter by the medicine man, right?"

"Yes," Gemma nodded.

"And you're saying that both sides of the family have cooperated with one another all these years?" I asked.

"Every one of them," Gemma said, "until your mama and I took you girls out of the picture. Maybe we were wrong. We thought we were protecting you. We can't change any of that now. What happens from here on out is up to you. Between what Myrtle will tell you, and what you'll find in this bag, you'll have your answers."

What Mom said next sent a shiver up my spine.

"No," she said softly, "they'll just know the right questions to start asking."

Before we left, Tori and Gemma stepped away and let me

have a moment alone with Mom. I put my hands on her arms. "I wish you'd told me," I said, "but I understand why you didn't."

"Thank you, Jinx," she said. "That means a lot to me."

"And, Mom?" I said, pulling her into a big hug. "I don't think you killed those girls. And even if you did, it wasn't what you meant to do. I love you."

A tremor passed through her body. She whispered in my ear, "I hope I didn't kill them, Norma Jean. But please be careful, Honey. I love you, too, and I don't ever want you to have to live with something like that. Magic is a huge responsibility. Don't ever forget that."

As Tori and I pulled away from the house, she said, "Are you okay?"

I nodded, but there was a knot in my throat that made it hard to speak.

"I had no idea," I finally managed to say.

"Me either," she replied, looking out the window.

We drove in silence for a couple of miles, and then I asked, "What did Gemma say when you guys left the room?"

"That she'll stay with your mom until your dad gets back," Tori answered.

Which is exactly what I expected, but it was still good to hear.

"So," I said, staring straight ahead at the road, "We talk to Myrtle?"

"Oh, *hell* yes," Tori said. "One way or another, we're getting the *whole* story this time."

My sentiments exactly.

3

Nothing about that day went the way we thought it would. We got back to the store a little after dark because we stopped to have a bite to eat. We weren't really hungry. That was just an excuse to recover from our conversation with the moms and to work up the nerve to speak with Myrtle.

Before we'd left to drive to Cotterville, Tori and I had debated about taking the time to unpack the boxes of supplies the UPS guy delivered the day before, but neither one of us was in the mood to get the job done. Since the boxes were gone, Darby must have tackled the chore for us.

Normally, when we came through the back door, he would have been waiting for us, but this time, the place was deserted. Then we saw the basement door standing ajar, casting a rectangle of light across the floor.

"Does that look like an invitation to you?" I asked Tori.

"Oh, yeah," she agreed. "Myrtle is a step ahead of us, as usual."

"Two steps," a woman's voice called from the basement. "Please come down and join us."

"Us?" I mouthed to Tori.

She shrugged, and gave me a silent, "Who knows?"

We did as we were told, and promptly got the surprise of our lives.

Myrtle was sitting in the "lair" under the stairs. The basement itself is filled with endless rows of industrial storage shelves four levels high. They extend as far as the eye can see, covering far more real estate than should be contained under the footprint of my store. Darby spends a great deal of time down there "cataloging" for Myrtle.

To be perfectly honest? I have *no* idea what the two of them are up to.

But in the corner under the stairs, Myrtle has created a workspace for us that looks like it belongs in an English manor house on some PBS show. The walls are covered in dark paneling, except for the space on either side of the fireplace. That's dominated by floor-to-ceiling-bookcases holding elegant old leather-bound books.

An oak table fills the center of the area, which is carpeted in beautiful Oriental rugs. Typically there are two leather wing-back chairs on either side of the fireplace, but we found three chairs holding three people--a brownie, and a rat.

I know. I know. The next line should be "walked into a bar."

Frankly? A drink probably was in order, but no one had yet shared with me that Myrtle keeps a cabinet full of single malt beside the roll top desk.

There was a cheerful little blaze in the fireplace. The basement is always several degrees colder than the upper floor. But that's not why an icy sensation went through my veins. Chase McGregor was sitting right there with Myrtle as if it were the most normal thing in the world.

Darby was perched on the arm of his chair, and there was a third, older man whom I didn't recognize. Rodney, our resident black-and-white domestic rat, was sleeping peacefully on the shoulder of Myrtle's gray sweater.

When Myrtle chose to appear to us in human form, she picked the most stereotypical librarian look you can imagine, including a gray bun high on her head secured with a yellow No. 2 pencil. She was now regarding us kindly from behind the round, black spectacles she didn't need, but which suited her new persona perfectly.

"Come sit with us," she said, gesturing to two empty chairs that completed the loose circle and were obviously meant for Tori and me.

When I remained frozen in place, Chase said nervously, "Please, Jinx. I know this is a shock, but we'll tell you everything if you'll just sit down."

He looked as sick to his stomach as I felt.

I looked at Myrtle, a note of accusation in my voice. "My mom called you, didn't she?"

"In a manner of speaking," Myrtle answered, unflappable as always. "It's been years since I've heard from Kelly. I was surprised she even remembered how to reach me, but she wanted to give me time to prepare."

"You mean to figure out how much you're willing to tell me?" I asked, trying not to give over to my rising anger, but the words were unmistakably hostile.

Half-truths were bad enough, but if Chase was sitting there, had I even been getting *quarter*-truths?

Here I'd been turning myself inside out to make certain he never saw anything strange in the shop, only to discover he was one of the people hiding things . . . no, not hiding, *lying*.

I thought Chase was trustworthy. So trustworthy, in fact, that I'd been losing sleep trying to figure out the best way to come clean with him about being a witch. I felt like a complete fool.

The sharpness of my question didn't phase Myrtle, who

continued to regard me placidly. "Don't be ridiculous," she said. "We have every intention of telling you the entire story. It is, however, rather a long tale. I think you'll be more comfortable if you join us."

Beside me, Tori said, in a low voice, "Come on, Jinksy. Hear them out."

In the end, however, it was the pleading look on Chase's face that finally made me move. Tori and I both sat down and I just looked at Myrtle. Waiting.

She sighed. "Very well then. I suppose your attitude is understandable. I'm afraid we have to start with a bit of a history lesson. Let me just say from the beginning that I am not beating around the proverbial bush. These facts are, what I believe is popularly referred to as, the 'backstory.'"

And it did go a ways "back" all right. Four-hundred-and-ninety-eight years to be exact.

Myrtle started in 1517 with the Protestant Reformation.

I had a vague, high-school-history-class memory of the Martin Luther story. He wrote up a bunch of objections to things Pope Leo X was doing and nailed the piece of paper on a church door. That's what passed for social media in the 16th century.

Basically, Luther's manifesto, *The 95 Theses*, made every highly placed Catholic in the church's power structure lose their minds. What Myrtle had to tell us from there, however, qualified as "the rest of the story."

In spite of my mood, I was fascinated.

For his day, Martin Luther really was a radical taking on the biggest "establishment" he could find. Luther objected to all kinds of things the Church in Rome was up to, and his ideas were dangerous in other ways.

Luther believed that the common people should be able to talk to God directly without a priest acting as a middleman, and he was an advocate of literacy. If people could read the Bible, they could make up their own minds about what the scriptures meant without waiting for the Pope to tell them.

Luther threatened the Church's monopoly on belief and learning, and *then* he went after the papal pocketbook. The Church made a lot of money selling "indulgences." Think of an indulgence as a holy hall pass. Wealthy sinners bought indulgences to knock a few years off the time they were likely to spend in purgatory after they died.

Purgatory is the place where folks who aren't headed straight to hell get tormented for a while before they're allowed to go to heaven. The bigger your sins, the longer the wait time. The Pope was making hefty cash selling his Get Out of Purgatory Free cards, but Luther called the whole business what it was, a scam.

That's all in the history books. What most people don't know is that at the same time Luther touched off the Protestant Reformation, there were similar events going on in the Fae world.

"Fae" is a sort of catchall term for all the magical races. You sometimes see them ... well, "us," I guess ... referred to as "The Folk," but the heavy Scot-Irish influence in our part of the world explains why the words Tori and I learned that day were all Gaelic with some Latin thrown in.

We already knew that there are "hereditary" witches and "made" witches, but those terms were a simplification. As we listened, Myrtle broke down the magical social order for us. The two big divisions are *Hereditarium Magicae* and *Creavit Magicae*.

Witches occupy a special place in the Fae world, which I'll help you understand in more or less the order it occurred to me to ask the question. That night, as I was listening to Myrtle talk, I honestly couldn't even allow myself to entertain the idea that I might not be "human," much less understand that my definition of what constitutes "humanity" needed some work. For now, let's just take this all one step at a time.

Magic is inherent in all creation. Some beings are simply born with the ability to access it. Like all power, however, magic can be corrupted through an act of *Proditor Magicae*. Rough translation, "*traitor magic.*"

An Hereditarium practitioner agrees to commit *Veneficus Trajectio*, the "poison transfer," to turn a mortal into a Creavit, a "created" or "made" witch. Generally, the mortal who seeks the transfer is looking to amass wealth, position, power, or all of the above, plus immortality. The one catch to the deal is that Creavit witches can't bear children. Brenna Sinclair was a Creavit witch.

What no one in the mortal world knew was that Martin Luther started the Protestant Reformation because he was under the spell of a Creavit witch. I mean seriously, let's just look at Luther's behavior. Then, the guy was considered a religious visionary. Today, he'd be handed a lifetime supply of the strongest antipsychotic on the market. Luther wrote theology sitting on the toilet and was known to fling his own . . . by-prod-ucts . . . at visions of the devil.

The Creavit practitioners behind the Reformation were quietly working to gain control of the royal courts of Europe. To accomplish that goal, they needed to dilute papal power. Within Fae society, one Hereditarium practitioner, a wizard from England, Barnaby Shevington, raised a protest not unlike Luther's objections to the Church of Rome.

According to Myrtle, the Ruling Elders governed the Fae in Europe. Shevington tried to oppose the rising power of the Creavit, saying they would never practice pure, natural magic because the stain of their mortal origins forever tainted them. The Creavit would, in his estimation, always use their powers for dark purposes.

Martin Luther was excommunicated for his troubles, and so was Barnaby Shevington. The Elders, whose numbers had been infiltrated by the Creavit, threatened him with the loss of his powers if he didn't back off. Shevington came up with a solution the Elders didn't anticipate. He founded a colony in the Americas.

In April 1584, Shevington and his Hereditarium followers sailed to the New World disguised as mortal settlers destined to build a colony on Chesapeake Bay on behalf of Sir Walter Raleigh. They arrived on Roanoke Island on the Outer Banks of North Carolina on July 4, where they were left alone for three years. When somebody finally got around to checking on them, there was nothing left of the settlement but a single skeleton. No other trace of the vanished colonists remained.

To this day, the Roanoke Island venture is referred to as "The Lost Colony," but they weren't lost at all. Shevington waited until the English ships were out of sight to head for the mountains of the interior where he built the first Fae colony in the New World.

Just as the Puritan settlers of New England came to this country to practice religious freedom (which really meant religion *their way*), Shevington and his followers wanted *magical* freedom. They immediately outlawed *Veneficius Trajectio* and, over time, their colony became a sanctuary for New and Old World Fae alike.

Yes, the Americas have their own magical population.

Ever heard of a dude named Sasquatch?

Critter called the chupacabra?

And you thought that stuff was just an old *X-Files* script.

Yeah. Me, too. But not anymore.

Myrtle handled the narrative right up to the point where Shevington marched off into the wilderness. Then she turned to Chase. He had listened to the whole story with his gaze firmly fixed on the pattern in the Oriental rug under his feet.

When Myrtle said, "I think you should tell her about Clan McGregor now," his head came up.

His eyes met mine and I felt an odd recognition. I had certainly looked into Chase's eyes before, but there was something in his gaze now that touched me in a different way. I just couldn't put my finger on what it was.

"Well," Chase began, "my ancestors came to the New World with Barnaby Shevington. You may have heard of our clan. Liam Neeson made a movie about one of my more illustrious kinsmen."

I frowned. "Rob Roy?" I asked.

"Yes," he said, "but my branch of the family has been in this country since 1584, so we missed out on the Battle of Culloden in 1746."

The expression on my face must have told him I had no idea what he was talking about, because he smiled and said, "It was a bad day for the Scots."

When I didn't say anything, he went on. "At any rate, the McGregors had a special mission in Shevington's plans for the New World, a mission we continue to fulfill to this day. We're . . . well . . . you see . . . we . . ."

Beside him the elderly man shifted restlessly in his chair and said tersely, "Oh, for God's sake, son. If you won't tell them, I will. The McGregors are werecats."

At the same time, Tori and I both said, "*Son?*"

The old fellow chuckled. "That's right. I'm Chase's father, Festus McGregor."

I stared at Chase. "You named your *cat* after your father?"

A slow blush spread over Chase's tanned cheeks. "Not exactly."

The old man said, "He didn't name the cat after me. I am the cat."

"Okay," I said, pushing up out of my chair, "I don't know what you all are up to, but I've had enough. This is just ridicu . . . "

"Fine," the old man grumbled. "I guess we have to play show and tell."

He stood up, stretching a little and giving to one leg. Then he sort of . . . shimmered. It started at the top of his head and pushed him down toward the floor. His flannel shirt and jeans pooled in a heap on the rug.

At first I thought he had disappeared entirely, and then a yellow head poked up out of the neck of the shirt. The Festus I *did* know, a ginger tomcat, extricated himself from the pile of clothes and fixed me with an appraising stare.

Then, as if we hadn't seen enough, he opened his mouth and said, very clearly, "Do you get it now?"

Puzzle pieces rocketed into place in my mind. I wheeled around and pointed an accusing finger at Chase.

"*You!*" I said. "*You* were the mountain lion at the waterfall and in the cemetery."

This time Chase turned scarlet to the roots of his hair, but he didn't look away. "Yes," he said quietly, "that was me. It's my job to protect you."

His *job*?

So *not* the right thing to say.

4

Whatever Chase read in my expression, he knew instantly he was in dangerous waters. The backpedaling started immediately. "I meant it's *Clan McGregor's* job to guard The Valley," he said hastily, "and the coven watching over Knasgowa's grave, which includes you . . . now . . . so that's why I used . . . why I said that . . ."

He trailed off miserably, fixing Myrtle with a mute appeal for help.

When she made no effort to jump in, Festus took pity on Chase and came to his son's rescue.

"Sit down, Jinx," the cat commanded, hobbling over to the hearth to get closer to the fire. "If you want to take your claws to my son when I'm done talking, no one will stop you."

"Gee. Thanks, Dad," Chase muttered.

As I watched, Festus turned in three tight, counterclockwise circles before settling down.

"Why do cats do that?" I asked curiously.

"We're not just cats," Festus said archly. "We're *Scots*. Three is a sacred number to Celtic peoples. It reflects the unity of mind, body, and spirit. McGregor cats turn three times to honor that belief."

I didn't fall off the bagpipe wagon yesterday. That just sounded too made up to believe.

"Okay. So why do *non-Scottish* cats do it then?" I countered.

Festus fixed me with an imperious glare. "Because they wish they *were* Scottish cats," he deadpanned.

"Right." I said sarcastically, "I'll run that by the next Siamese I see and get back to you."

Myrtle stifled a giggle and Chase got very interested in the toes of his boots again.

Tori, however, was so juiced that we were sitting there having a conversation with a *cat*, she simply could not repress her enthusiasm.

"This is just so *awesome*," she said, in a tone of voice that sounded perilously close to gushing. "Why are you a house cat and Chase is a mountain lion?"

I wanted to know the answer to that one, too.

"Finally," Festus groused, "an intelligent question. I am a house cat because I am *retired*. After I hurt my leg, I couldn't patrol anymore. I can't very well lounge in the sunlight on my bench as a mountain lion, now, can I?"

Hard point to argue.

Then it occurred to me how many times I'd sat on that bench with Festus scratching his ears.

I had scratched Chase's father's ears.

Oh. My. God.

Taking a deep breath, and trying to shove that thought as far out of my mind as possible, I made an effort to get back on track.

"You said it's your job to guard a valley. What valley?"

"Shevington's Valley," Festus answered.

Why on earth would that valley need to be guarded, unless. .

.

"You can't possibly be suggesting that Shevington's settlement is still out . . . there," I said, gesturing in the general directions of the mountains.

Festus considered my statement for a moment, and then pointed with one front paw. "It's more like over *there*," he said, "but actually the valley exists in the place in between."

The place in between?

What the *heck* was that supposed to mean?

The magical doublespeak was bad enough, but coming from the mouth of a talking cat who was my kind-of boyfriend's father? This was all getting to be too much for me.

I sat back down heavily.

"Okay," I said with resignation, "I'm listening."

Festus reached up with his good back leg to contemplatively scratch his ear. "You like old movies, don't you?" he finally asked.

"How did you . . . "

OMG 2.0.

Festus had been right there in the cobbler's shop listening to every conversation Chase and I had. The old rascal had *watched* while we kissed. Now it was my turn to blush.

The cat chuckled when he saw me redden. "Yes, I'm a terrible eavesdropper," he admitted, "but I'm not a voyeur. I left the room when the two of you started rubbing whiskers."

Now *there* was a euphemism I'd never heard before.

I decided for the most neutral response possible.

"Yes," I said, pretending to ignore everything after the movie question, "I like old films."

"So you've seen *Brigadoon*?" Festus asked.

The 1954 MGM musical with Gene Kelly, Van Johnson, and Cyd Charisse was one of my mom's favorites. The plot is about an idyllic Scottish village that only appears once every 100 years.

"Yes," I said, "I've seen *Brigadoon*. So you're telling me this Valley of Shevington blips in and out of the real world?"

Festus shook his head. "No," he said, "I'm telling you that time runs along different streams. If it's easier, think of time like radio frequencies."

"You mean the way you can sometimes *almost* tune in a station?" Tori said.

"Exactly," Festus said. "The Valley of Shevington exists in a different stream of time that the Fae have the ability to access. That's how The Valley has remained undetected for centuries."

"Then why does it need to be guarded?" I asked.

"A mortal can only get to The Valley in the company of a member of one of the magical races," Festus explained, "but the entrances are vulnerable to Creavit witches."

So, there *had* been bigger stakes involved back in the day when Alexander Skea and Knasgowa went to such great lengths to keep Brenna Sinclair out of Briar Hollow.

"What would a Creavit witch stand to gain from reaching The Valley?" Tori asked.

Festus looked at Myrtle. "I think you should answer that."

Without hesitation, Myrtle said, "The last Alchemist lives there. She is the only surviving practitioner who knows how to perform *Veneficus Trajectio.*"

"What's an Alchemist?" I asked.

"The Alchemists were a special class of Fae," Myrtle replied. "Their ranks were drawn from many races within our world. In some of our cultures, they were called Druids. Perhaps you've heard of Merlin?"

I thought Tori's eyes were going to pop right out of her head.

"No way," she gasped.

Under any other circumstances, I would have laughed when Myrtle answered, "Yes way," but I was starting to feel a little shell-shocked.

"It doesn't really matter what you call them," she continued. "That's just semantics. From the 12th century forward, the

Alchemists worked to codify and preserve the esoteric knowledge of our kind. Many of the terms we use are Latin because it was the learned language of the time."

"And there's only one Alchemist left?" Tori asked.

Myrtle nodded. "Yes," she said. "As the Creavit gained more power in Europe, the Alchemists fled to The Valley of Shevington and sought sanctuary there."

Which explained the protection part. I looked at Festus. "The werecats patrol the mountains?"

He nodded. "That's why there are so many legends about panthers in these hills."

"My granny, Dad's mom, called them 'painters,'" Tori said. "She told me a painter screams like a woman."

Festus drew up with pride. "In my day I could let out with a scream that would curdle the blood in your veins."

"You used the legends and the screams to keep people out of the deep mountains," I said.

Festus nodded. "Between us and the Brown Mountain lights, people have stayed at a distance for generations."

If you've never heard of them, the Brown Mountain lights appear over by Linnville. People call them "ghost lights." They've been studied for decades, but no one has ever come up with a solid explanation for the flashes that light up the night sky near Brown Mountain.

Darby, who had been silent throughout the whole conversation, mumbled something. The only word I caught was "fairy."

"What did you say, Darby?" I asked.

Looking a little shamefaced, Darby answered. "I said the fairies are terrible showoffs, Mistress," he said.

He sounded like the class nerd who never got to hang out with the cool kids.

"The Brown Mountain lights are fairies," Myrtle explained. "They conduct military drills in the vicinity of Brown Mountain at night to further divert attention from the area around Briar Hollow."

I covered my eyes with my hand and shook my head. "*Please* tell me that's all of it," I pleaded.

Which, of course, it wasn't.

There was no time for me to process if the next part was good news or bad, because Myrtle just put it out there. We could get to The Valley of Shevington by passing through the basement.

I looked up at her. "My mother told me you are aos sí," I said. "What does that mean?"

Myrtle's gaze locked on mine. Suddenly she was no longer an old librarian. Instead, we were looking at the most radiantly beautiful woman I had ever seen. She was tall and thin, with thick, golden hair falling down around her shoulders. Her face glowed with an inner light and her voice carried the lilt of running water when she spoke.

Rodney slipped away from her shoulders and scampered down to the floor, bowing low before her.

"I was old when the earth was young," she said softly. "I, too, inhabit the space in between, but I exist to help all the races, mortal and Fae alike. Some have called me a goddess, but that I am not. I came here to this land with Barnaby Shevington. I passed through the earth under the cold, dark waters of the Atlantic and made a new home in these hills. I am counselor and friend to thee, Jinx Hamilton. I am sister and mother. I am as I have always been and as I will always be."

Then the glow was gone, and I was once again looking into the kind face of the woman Myrtle chose to show us every day. She held her hand out to Rodney.

"Arise, little one," she commanded gently. In response, Rodney climbed back up the sleeve of her sweater and cuddled against her neck.

"Do you believe me now, Jinx?" she asked.

Beside me, I felt Darby's tiny hand slip into mine. I looked down into his honest, wizened face. "Believe, Mistress," he said. "The Valley is a good place, and you have much to learn there."

I looked over at Tori, who nodded her head. I looked at Chase, whose eyes begged me not to think ill of him. I looked at Festus, silhouetted against the fire.

It was just all too much at one time.

Standing up, I said, "Give me some time . . . alone."

For just a second a flicker of hurt passed through Tori's eyes, but then she nodded again and smiled. "Call me if you need me," she said.

"Always," I whispered, and then I left.

I didn't look back as I walked up the steps. My keys were still in my pocket. I went straight out the back door, got in my car, and headed for the cemetery. There was only one person I wanted to talk to at that moment. Beau Longworth.

5

M y plan to drive straight to the cemetery didn't work out. At the edge of town, I pulled off to the side of the road, cut the engine, and rolled down the window. My heart felt like it was about to hammer right out of my chest and a fine sheen of perspiration covered my face. The night was warm, but the waves of heat washing over me didn't come from the atmosphere. Now, I know that both my magic and my emotions reeled that night, but in the moment, I honestly thought I might be having a heart attack.

A gentle breeze from the window soothed my blazing skin, but it wasn't enough. Suddenly the car seemed too small and too airless. My throat closed down and I gasped to find air. Fighting against the handle like a caged animal, I threw open the door and half fell out on the ground.

My knees struck rough gravel, and the pain was just enough to open a small window through the maelstrom in my mind. I closed my eyes and tried to send that tiny anchor of calm out along my jangled nerves. An image of my mother's eyes filled my thoughts, the memory of her sadness and fear twisting at my gut.

Sooner or later, I think most of us realize that we've judged our parents unfairly. Mom and I didn't necessarily have a *bad* relationship up to that day, but I had always been closer to my dad. But as I thought of my mother, confessing the horrible secret she'd carried for so many years with tears coursing down her cheeks, I was ashamed of myself.

Gemma was right. I didn't have any idea what my mother had gone through in life. I just took the path of least resistance and gravitated toward my dad because he was *easier*. I had always thought Mom had too many rules, too many "right ways" to do things.

I resented her nervous, cautious approach to the world because it rubbed off on me when I was younger. As an adult, I worked hard to curb those tendencies or I really might have turned into one of those people who can't leave their homes. Agoraphobia, I think it's called.

Tori and my job at Tom's Cafe get equal credit for helping to ensure my comfort zone didn't narrow down to an anxious cage. Tori has always been one great big adventure waiting to happen, and there's nothing like working in a busy local eatery to keep you involved in the daily life of a community.

The thought of the regulars at Tom's sent a pang of longing through me. I used to love to walk into the cafe in the dark, pre-dawn hours. The transition from darkness to bright lights at the start of a new day never failed to perk up my sleepy spirits. The breakfast crowd guzzled a gallon or two of coffee while filling us in on the rumor du jour. By supper, we'd be giggling privately over how the same story had transformed and expanded in just a few hours.

Even though there's a lot about being a waitress that's just hot, dirty, and exhausting, I had fun at Tom's. It wasn't the kind of job that was going to help me realize any major life goals, but it taught me to work hard, take responsibility for my actions, and appreciate the value of a dollar.

Tip big people. That's a hard working person setting that plate down in front of you.

There's no question that I grew up in Tom's and toughened up.

But that night, on my knees on the side of the road in the dark, I grew up even more. I was filled with empathy for my mom, hiding what she suspected was the truth about how those high school girls died. Living with that every day. Knowing that no one would believe her even if she had tried to confess.

Those realizations brought my mom's way of being in the world into much sharper focus for me. All of her nervous clucking pointed to one central fact of her existence; she was terrified of ever doing anything that would hurt someone again. And she found the idea of my using magic too frightening to even comprehend.

In her own way, Mom had always been trying to protect me. She couldn't see that by not telling me the truth, she'd left me open and vulnerable. Now, all the people around me -- the ones who knew how much information I really needed -- seemed to be doing the same thing. It was driving me absolutely insane.

Which sent me right into a completely paradoxical meltdown. I had wanted -- no, *demanded* -- to be told everything. I really didn't have a lot of room to complain that the answers I was given were just too much. Everyone back in that basement cared about me. I was pretty sure they all loved me, but in their heads I was already some kind of super witch.

That night on the side of the road listening to the night sounds, I wanted the world to stop ... expanding ... until I could catch up. Darby asked me to believe. The problem was, I did believe, I just didn't know what to *do* with that belief yet.

Magical powers. Ghosts. Alternate history. Heck, alternate

time. I think a girl can be forgiven for letting herself have a panic attack. Part of me felt as if I've been lied to my entire life, and another part of me was disappointed in not having been asked to join the party sooner.

As for the revelation that Chase was a werecat, I couldn't even begin to process that one. Was he really interested in me or had he just been doing his job all along? The way he was looking at me when I left the basement, I liked to think he wanted to know me, the woman, not me, the witch. But could those two things even be separated anymore?

When my hands stopped shaking and the hammering of my heart subsided, I slowly got to my feet, bracing myself with both hands against the roof of the Prius. When I felt steady enough to be behind the wheel, I got in and drove the rest of the way to the cemetery.

I found Beau near the marble obelisk that marks his final resting place. He was tossing a ghostly tennis ball for Duke, a particularly incongruous sight, since Beau was buried in his Confederate colonel's uniform.

The graveyard was almost deserted. There were only a few other spectres present, but none of them were close to Beau's grave. Now that the resident spirits can come and go as they please, they have a tendency to wander into town. Some check on loved ones and others just like to see the 21st century world.

Beau greeted me with his usual gallantry, bending to kiss my hand even though he couldn't touch me here. Had we been at the store, where Myrtle's power amplified his energy, I would have felt the cool press of his lips on my skin.

As he straightened up, Beau frowned slightly. "You are upset, Miss Jinx," he said, concern filling his words. "What has happened?"

I almost asked him if he had time to talk to me, which would have been ridiculous. The dead have nothing but time on their hands. I had intended to calmly recite everything that happened. Instead it all came pouring out in a jumbled torrent of words.

When I started crying, Beau reached for the breast pocket of his coat to hand me his handkerchief, and then realized the gesture was impossible. Seeing how much he wanted to comfort me but couldn't only made me cry harder.

When I finally ran out of steam and choked out, ". . . and so I came here to talk to you," Beau said with infinite gentleness, "Please don't cry any more, you will make yourself quite ill. Come, sit with me and we will talk."

He ushered me over to a granite bench intended for the mourners of the late S. Scholtemeyer, but since he or she left this life in 1897, I didn't think anyone would mind if Beau and I had a seat.

"I must admit that I am quite astounded by the things you have told me," Beau began, "but given the current nature of my own being, I am somewhat more tolerant of the fantastical than I might have been when I was alive."

Beau has an immense capacity for understatement.

"That's why I wanted to talk to you," I sniffled. "You're the only person I know whose world got all turned upside down, too."

In spite of himself, Beau chuckled. "My dear," he said, "death is, perhaps, the ultimate redefinition. Be thankful you have been spared a transformation of that magnitude."

I had to give him that. Aunt Fiona always said that any day when you wake up alive is a good day.

"So, what did you do?" I asked. "When you realized everything you thought you knew about your existence had suddenly changed?"

Beau stretched his long legs away from the bench. Even

though he was almost transparent to me, I could see the scratches and wear on the leather of his high cavalry boots.

"I did what all spirits do when they awaken to this new reality," Beau said. "I looked for the most ordinary thing I could still do and clung to that as if it were a life preserver."

"What was that thing?"

"Walking," he said. "Before the war, I heard a young man named Henry Thoreau deliver a lecture on the virtues of walking. Like him, I have always cleaved to the soul-cleansing potential of a vigorous hike. Although I could not leave the boundaries of this place, I walked the grounds each night, searching my conscience for an understanding of why I was here or simply enjoying the distraction of my own momentum. The body changes, Miss Jinx, but the mind remains intact. I slowly learned to continue my life in the realm of my own intellect. Then, gradually, as other restless spirits came to reside here, I resumed my lifelong calling to be of service to others. I tried, in so far as I was able, to be a leader and a mediator."

He found a way to continue being who he had always been regardless of his circumstances.

When I didn't say anything, Beau asked, "Do you know your Shakespeare, my dear?"

"Just enough to pass senior English in high school," I admitted.

"'This above all: to thine own self be true,'" Beau quoted. "'And it must follow, as the night the day, Thou canst not then be false to any man.'"

I wished Mrs. Florsheim had been that good at relating Shakespeare to real life. I would have enjoyed her class a whole lot more.

"You're telling me I can handle all this if I just keep being myself," I said.

At just that moment, Duke loped up and dropped a glowing

tennis ball at Beau's feet. The Colonel stooped down, retrieved the ball, and sent it flying over the gravestones with Duke in hot pursuit.

"Exactly, my dear," he smiled. "Death has hardly stopped Duke from being a dog, now has it?"

I laughed and wished with all my heart I could hug him. "Thank you, Beau," I said. "So much."

"Seek solace in the known, Miss Jinx," Beau said. "Open your shop tomorrow. Go about your business. Take the time you need to assimilate the new world that is opening before you into your understanding. Let no one else define that readiness for you, and all will be well."

"That's really good advice," I said. "Today we'd say just get off the rollercoaster."

"I don't know what this is," Beau conceded, "but the context sounds in keeping with the point I am attempting to make."

Off to my left, an owl hooted. When I glanced up in that direction, I suddenly realized the night sky was alive with stars. I could even see the Milky Way. It was breathtakingly beautiful and incredibly peaceful.

"Can I just stay here with you and Duke for now?" I asked, as the departed coonhound trotted up to us again.

"We would both be delighted with the pleasure of your company," Beau said, reaching to catch the ball the dog dropped in his hand. "Duke is quite prepared for this game of fetch to last for eternity."

6

The group in the basement

No one spoke after Jinx asked for time alone to think. She climbed the stairs, her footsteps echoing on the floor over their heads. Then they heard the back door open and close.

Chase looked over at Tori. "Is she going to be all right?" he asked.

Tori was torn between a strong desire to lay into him for being clueless and sympathizing with his obvious remorse.

"Jinx needs some time to process," she said. "This was a lot to get hit with in one day. Honestly, guys, couldn't you have managed all of this a little better? The shock and awe approach was kinda brutal."

Myrtle sighed. "I assure you we would have preferred to handle the entire matter in a completely different and slower way," she said, "but Jinx was a bit ambitious with her use of magic at the cemetery. Frankly, none of us imagined she had enough control to perform a spell of the magnitude necessary to release Brenna Sinclair. Those events accelerated our timetable so to speak. Without formal training, facing Brenna was a brilliant, although foolish, feat. We can't afford to let anything like that happen again."

"Uh, excuse me," Tori said, "but I was kinda in on all that, too."

Myrtle smiled. "You have proven to be a bit of a surprise as well."

Mollified, Tori gestured toward the shelves. "Am I right in assuming that everything down here has something to do with training Jinx?" she asked.

"With training you both," Myrtle said.

Tori eyed her suspiciously. "You've known all along that I'm descended from Alexander and Knasgowa, haven't you?"

Myrtle nodded. "Yes," she said, "I have."

"So why the big act?" Tori asked. "Why the whole thing with the scrying and the necklace?"

"To put it bluntly," Myrtle said, "we were testing you."

"Because I'm descended from a Creavit witch?" Tori asked. "What? You thought as soon as I found out I'd go all traitor or something?"

"We took the same precautions with you that were taken with every one of your forbearers," Myrtle said. "You may ask your mother for confirmation of that. The Creavit element is always an unknown."

Tori leaned forward in her chair, resting her elbows on her knees. "You know what, Myrtle?" she said. "I like you. I like you a lot. But you should get one thing straight that will never be an 'unknown.' Jinx is my sister. My loyalty is to her. Period. I don't care what's running around in my bloodstream. Got it?"

"Got it," Myrtle said. "I would have expected nothing less, because those are virtually the same words Gemma used when we tested her loyalty to Kelly. Surely you can understand, however, that we have a great deal to protect."

Tori frowned. "Wait a minute," she said. "What do you mean you tested Mom and her loyalty to Kelly?"

"As a young woman," Myrtle said, "Kelly exhibited the same potential as her daughter, but as you have learned, she made a mistake from which she could not recover."

"But they told us that they weren't very powerful," Tori said. "Are you saying they lied?"

Myrtle shook her head. "No," she said, "they told you that with which they are comfortable believing. Had they completed their training, they would have been a formidable partnership."

"Trust me," Tori said, "with or without magic, Mom and Kelly are a dynamic duo."

Myrtle inclined her head in agreement and Tori went on. "So, let me see if I've got this straight. Jinx is powerful, but together, we're the mother lode? That's what happened when we mixed our blood at the cemetery, wasn't it?"

"Yes," Myrtle said.

"Okay," Tori bristled, "would it have been too freaking much to tell us about the blood thing *before* we had to do that whole *West Side Story* remake?"

From the hearth, Festus chuckled. "I think you're going to have your hands full with this one, Myrtle," he said. "She has claws."

"You have no idea," Tori said.

Myrtle chuckled. "I suspect I do have an idea," she said, "she is very like her mother. Now, as for the matter of the blood, had I told you, you might have over-thought the situation. Blood magic must be awakened by genuine need. When you require the power again, a mere pin prick will suffice."

"Good to know," Tori said, "and I'm holding you to that."

"Noted," Myrtle said. "Now, so that I may more fully explain your situation, if you will indulge me, where do you think we are at the moment?"

Tori's eyes wandered up the staircase and then tracked around the room. "I think," she said finally, "that when we come down the staircase we go through some kind of doorway or something. You've got it set up so only certain people can come through. The old basement, the one filled with all the junk is still here, taking up the same space, but like Festus said, on a different frequency. If there's a way to get to The Valley from here, then I think we're in the place in between."

Darby clapped his hands, and then sheepishly buried them in his pockets when Myrtle looked at him over her glasses.

"I'm guessing I'm right," Tori grinned.

"For the most part, yes," Myrtle said. "And your answer is quite astute. This is one level of the place in between, a sort of transition, if you will, to The Valley. It is necessary to pass through another doorway, as you call it, to reach Shevington proper. That entrance is also warded."

Tori frowned. "Warded?" she asked. "Doesn't that mean you've cast some kind of spell on the stairs?"

Myrtle nodded approvingly. "You are a quick study," she said. "There are precisely 9 beings other than myself that can enter the place you think of as the basement."

Still frowning, Tori counted off on her fingers. "Me, Jinksy, Darby, Festus, Chase, Rodney, Aunt Fiona, and Colonel Long-worth," she said. "Those are all the people I've ever seen down here. Who's the ninth?"

A voice from the stacks said, "I am."

Amity Prescott stepped into the carpeted area and sat down in the chair Jinx had vacated. "Hi, Tori," she said. "Quite a day you gals are having, huh?"

Tori stared at her for a second and then she snapped her fingers. "The Briar Hollow coven?" she asked.

Amity smiled. "Guilty," she said. "I wanted to reveal myself to you and Jinx when the whole business with the cemetery ghosts was going on, but Fiona wouldn't let me. She was right. If you girls had needed my help, it would have been better for Brenna not to know about me in advance. But you all did just fine."

"For two people who had no earthly clue what they were doing," Tori said wryly.

Amity turned to Myrtle. "Since Jinx isn't here, can I assume she's having a little trouble coping with the . . . bigger picture?"

Before Myrtle could answer, Chase sighed heavily, "That and the revelation she's been more or less dating an alley cat."

Festus arched his back indignantly. "We are not *alley* cats," he hissed.

Tori intervened. "Look, Festus, I'm a huge fan of all things feline and so is Jinx. This is not a species thing," she said. "Jinx doesn't like men lying to her. She's been there, done that, and grabbed the t-shirt. More than once."

It was Chase's turn for indignation. "I'm not one of those guys," he protested.

Without blinking, Tori said, "Did you or didn't you lie to her?"

Chase set his jaw stubbornly. "Only by omission," he said.

"*Oh!*" Tori said. "I see. We're going to do the whole *shades* of truth thing. That should fix things right up. *Not.*"

Chase opened his mouth to answer, then closed it again, and looked to Myrtle for help.

"I'm sorry, Chase," Myrtle said, "but I'm afraid I have to agree with Tori. I told you that you needed to tell Jinx about yourself. In fact, we all told you, and you insisted you needed more time. I'm afraid that time has caught up with you."

"That's not fair," Chase said angrily. "How exactly was I supposed to tell her I'm a werecat? How do you work that into a casual dinner conversation?"

"By just telling her," Tori said. "Let me give you a real good piece of advice, Chase. If you do manage to get back in her good graces, I don't suggest you underestimate Jinx again. She's a big girl. She would have much rather heard the werecat thing directly from you. Weeks ago. I know her. She's out there trying to decide if you like her for herself or if you've just been spending time with her because it's your job."

The flush returned to Chase's features. "Of course I like her for herself, but it's not that easy."

The comment hung in the air. Tori looked around the room.

"Okay, spill," she said, "what are you all not telling me?"

Festus let out a little rasping cough as if he were clearing a hairball out of his throat. Then, in a completely matter-of-fact tone, he said, "Typically we only mate with our own kind."

"*Whoa, whoa, whoa!*" Tori said. "Throw it in reverse there, Garfield. *Mating?*"

Chase glared at his father. "What Dad meant to say is that traditionally, werecats only date other werecats. No member of our clan has ever been involved with a witch, and we're not certain the . . . power sets . . . would be compatible. Even pairings with humans have unpredictable results."

"The children could have tails," Festus offered helpfully.

Tori's eyes widened a little. "Uh, yeah, okay. Let's hold off on telling Jinx about that until she's a little more down with the whole turning furry thing, okay?"

"Not. A. Problem," Chase assured her. "But that is *not* the reason I didn't tell her about myself," he added. "I wanted her to get to know me as a person first."

Tori shook her head. "And she wanted you to get to know her as a person before she told you that she's a witch," she said. "The two of you are some pair."

"So have I completely blown any chance I have with her?" Chase asked somberly. "Should I go try to find her?"

Without hesitation, Tori said, "No, that would be a huge mistake. I don't think you've necessarily blown it, but do *not* push her, Chase. Give her some space. Let me talk to her. Jinksy isn't good with change, and she's had way too much of it this summer. She's overwhelmed."

Myrtle nodded. "I agree," she said. "And besides, I can sense Jinx's power signature. She's in the cemetery talking with Colonel Longworth. She's perfectly fine."

Chase breathed a long sigh of relief. "Good," he said, "that makes me a feel a little better."

Myrtle turned back toward Tori. "Now," she said, "to resume our conversation. As I said, you are for the most part correct about our location. We are inside what is technically called a fairy mound. It is my home and the place where The Valley of Shevington maintains its archives and library. The Valley has not only served as a sanctuary for the Fae, but also as a repository for Fae scholarship. Many powerful artifacts of our culture reside here for safekeeping."

"Which is why you dress up like a librarian," Tori said. "You went with the theme."

"It seemed an appropriate persona," Myrtle said, "one that both you and Jinx would find acceptable."

"So, if Jinx is supposed to be this big deal witch," Tori said, "and I'm supposed to have powers of my own, what am I?"

Darby held his hand up, which won him a bemused smile from Myrtle. "What is it, Darby?" she asked.

"Please, Your Majesty," he asked excitedly, "may I have the honor of telling Mistress Tori what she is?"

Myrtle nodded gravely. "Proceed," she said.

With barely contained glee, Darby said breathlessly, "Mistress Tori, you are the next Alchemist!"

7

W hen I got back to the store in the wee hours of the morning, the door of Tori's apartment was ajar and her light was on. Feeling distinctly like I was standing outside my parents' bedroom door getting in late from a date to the football game, I called out softly, "I'm home, Mom."

Tori appeared at the door in sleep shorts and an over-sized *Star Wars* t-shirt with Chewbacca in Hank Williams, Jr. shades emblazoned with the words "Party Animal."

"Hey," she said. "I went up and fed the cats, so don't buy it when they try to convince you they're starving."

"Thanks," I said. "Would I be a real jerk if I asked you to open up in the morning?"

"Naw," she grinned. "I'm good with the breakfast shift."

Since we opened the espresso bar, we'd been turning on the lights and unlocking the door around 7 o'clock, just to see if anyone might wander in. They wandered in all right, in droves, with newspapers and tablets. The first couple of days several customers made a point of thanking me for the blazing-fast free wifi.

One woman in particular, a summer resident who rented a

house a block off the square, said enthusiastically, "I don't know how you do it. You must pay the earth for speeds that fast."

As soon as she was out the door, I dragged Tori into the storeroom and whispered furiously, "Free high-speed wifi?! Are you out of your mind? We can't afford that!"

She held up her hand to stop me. "Myrtle takes care of it," she said simply.

Talk about unlimited MBPS.

Between that, and Darby's custom blended grinds, we were a hit from day one. Darby was already begging me to let him supply baked goods, which I had every intention of doing, as soon as I figured out how to sell it to the Health Department. We'd have to have a kitchen to convince the inspector that normal food prep was going on, but Darby was in the Easy Bake Oven class.

The bar's seating area started out with six mismatched tables of varying sizes, but we'd just added two more, as well as a couple of beat-up "vintage" armchairs. The more casual, over-flow customers just camped on the first few levels of the stairs leading up to my apartment.

Long story short, as much as I'd thought my early morning waitressing days were over, that was proving not to be the case.

That night I thanked Tori for being willing to take care of opening up, and then said, a little lamely, "Guess I'll turn in."

"You've been crying," Tori said.

"Yeah," I admitted. "I went on a regular jag with Beau."

"Poor guy," Tori said. "I'll bet he almost went nuts trying to hand you a handkerchief."

"Pretty much," I admitted.

"Did he help?"

"He did," I said. "He suggested I just concentrate on normal things until I'm ready to think about all the ... other ... stuff."

"That's good advice," Tori said. "You go on up and get some

sleep. I'll take care of the store. Don't worry about coming down until you're ready."

Impulsively, I reached out and gave her a fierce hug.

"Did I do something huggable," Tori asked when I held on tight, "or do you just really need a hug?"

"Both," I mumbled. "We'll talk tomorrow. Okay?"

"Whenever you're ready."

I let her go, took a few steps toward the stairs, and stopped. "Is Chase okay?" I asked softly.

"He feels like an idiot for not telling you sooner," Tori said. "And he's worried about you. We all are."

"I'm okay," I said. "I just need a little time to adjust to . . . everything."

"That's what I told them," she said. "The magical freight train is gonna slow down until you're ready to ride."

When I reached the top of the landing, I heard Tori's door close. I glanced back over my shoulder and stopped in my tracks. For just an instant, I thought I saw something whizz past the bottom of the stairs, which were dimly lit by the nightlight we left burning by the storeroom door just in case either of us had to move around the store at night.

I started down to check out what I'd seen, and then it occurred to me it might be what we euphemistically call a "water bug" in the south. That's a nice way of saying "big ole flying cockroach." Most of them are large enough to saddle, and they'll make you hurt yourself they're so disgusting and prone to dive bomb right in your face.

For the record, said repulsive insects live in trees, but they get in houses all the time. I've never seen one upstairs, but then I live with four furry pest control agents.

Deciding to leave well enough alone, I made a mental note to get some industrial strength roach traps. I'd already had more than I could stand for one night anyway. A water bug doing a kamikaze imitation could well have brought on a heart attack.

I should have gone straight to bed as soon as I let myself in the apartment. It was late, or really early, depending on how you wanted to look at it. I was tired, but my mind wouldn't slow down. Rather than lie there in the dark listening to my churning thoughts, I followed Beau's advice. I did ordinary things.

First, I played with the cats, and then I straightened up after we made a mess of the living room. The dishwasher needed to be emptied and there was laundry to fold. At one point I wandered in front of the standing mirror in my bedroom and just stared at myself.

Did I look like a witch? When I passed people on the street, did they whisper behind my back? "Oh, yeah. That one's a witch. Totally." I leaned in and looked suspiciously at the end of my nose. No warts. Yet.

No one who knew me would ever have described me as an ambitious person. I think that's how it is for a lot of people. You get out of high school and according to how much money your folks have, or how willing you are to carry student loan debt, you float into something. Even the kids with a plan are likely to change majors once they find out they don't actually like the "career" they've been talking about since grade school.

My parents don't have a lot of money, and I didn't want to start out my adult life with tens of thousands of dollars in debt. Consequently, I didn't spend a lot of time thinking about my purpose in life. I just tried to work hard, be decent to other people, and make a little place for myself.

Now I was part of something bigger than I'd ever imagined -- something that had been going on for hundreds of years.

Let me jump ahead a few hours and tell you that the next morning I woke up ready to fully embrace my new role in life. Happy to embrace that role, in fact. What got me there?

Tales of a hidden city in a mountain valley existing in another stream of time?

Finding out my boyfriend was a werecat, which, if I'm going to be honest, was kind of hot?

Living atop a fairy mound and hanging out with an ancient animating spirit?

No, no, and no.

While I was standing there looking at myself in the mirror, I caught sight of the satchel Mom gave me earlier in the day. I refused to carry it for fear my psychometry might kick in. Tori had apparently brought it up when she fed the cats earlier and left it on the foot of my bed.

I went over and cautiously laid my hand on the worn leather. Opening my mind just a little, I "tasted" the energy. That's really the only word I can use. The flavor was aged by time; mellowed, cured, and so familiar it seemed to flow out of the bag and up into my body.

The brass snaps were cool under my fingers as I undid them and lifted the flap. The interior of the satchel was filled with papers, notebooks, and envelopes, but a single bundle caught my eye. It was a scrap of simple blue cotton, neatly folded, and tied with a red satin ribbon.

The knot in the ribbon slid smoothly apart when I tugged gently on one end. The crimson length slid free and pooled around the cotton. When I carefully unfolded the fabric, I found a white lace handkerchief, delicate as the web of a spider. In one corner, embroidered in ecru thread, were the initials "JDS."

With some real genealogical work behind me now, I can tell you that the letters stand for Johanna Dawson Shaw, my great-great-grandmother on Mom's side of the family. She was born in 1875. That night I knew nothing about her, but without a moment's hesitation, I gently picked up the handkerchief, letting it rest whisper light on the palm of my hand.

Closing my eyes, I instantly found myself in the store, as it had been more than a hundred years before. Myrtle was there, in her true form, the one she revealed to me earlier that night. And also there were 13 other women; the Briar Hollow Coven.

They weren't witches in pointy hats. They weren't wizened crones with warts and green skin like the witch on the mystery cup someone had left on our doorstep. They were women with work-roughened hands and faces. Their eyes told me they had known the joy of birth and the crushing loss of death.

Sitting together in a circle, many with bits of needlework in their hands, they talked and laughed. I was reminded of something Beau told me once about his wife, how she and her friends read books and discussed politics all under the guise of being a crocheting circle.

I suddenly understood what women of ability had done through generations to survive in the world, to retain something of themselves while they fulfilled their roles as wives and mothers. There was power in that circle, but it wasn't just the power of magic. It was the power of sisterhood.

Myrtle sat with them, ancient and wise, being for them what she said she would be for me -- counselor and friend, sister and mother. It wasn't just the aos sí that had been old when the earth was young; it was this ineffable essence of womankind.

In my vision each of the women turned to look at me, warming me with their kindness and their acceptance. But it was Johnna who spoke, "This is your birthright, child. Seize it and take your place among us."

Just as suddenly as I had been transported through time, I was back sitting on the edge of my bed with the scrap of lace in my hand. I felt calm, safe, and suddenly tired, but in a good way. The kind of tired you feel when you've worked hard and done something right.

After carefully rewrapping the handkerchief and tying the

satin ribbon back in place, I put the satchel away, climbed into bed and fell into a peaceful sleep. The next morning I awakened to glorious, golden sun streaming through the front windows. All the cats were curled up on the foot of the bed, purring in unison. Glancing at the clock on the bedside table, I was shocked to see it was 8:30. The cats *never* let me sleep late.

"What gives, guys?" I asked, peering down at them.

Four contented and all-knowing gazes met my own.

"You feel the magic, too, don't you?" I said. "My little herd of familiars. Does that mean you don't want cat food?"

At those last two words, four sets of ears went instantly alert.

"Yeah," I said, throwing back the covers, "that's what I thought."

Even though I was in no particular hurry, it was just after 9 o'clock when I came bouncing down the stairs. The tables in the espresso bar were all full. I exchanged greetings with several customers and stepped behind the counter to say good morning to Tori.

"You look good today," she said, eyeing me critically. "What's up with that?"

"I had a look inside that satchel Mom gave us," I said, pouring myself a cup of coffee. "And it was a . . . visionary . . . experience."

We couldn't talk directly for fear of being overheard, but Tori knew instantly what I meant. "I take it you're happier about the direction of things?" she asked cryptically.

"Yes," I said with firm conviction. "I think we should meet again with the . . . group . . . tonight. Sound good?"

Tori grinned. "Sounds good, because there were a few things that happened after you left the meeting last night that you should know about."

Color me shocked.

"How about I go down to George and Irma's and get us a bag

of doughnuts," I said. "We can hide in the storeroom and you can tell me about it."

"Deal," Tori said. "If anybody wants anything, they can ring the bell."

Still keeping my voice low, I said, "You didn't find anything large and insectoid down here this morning, did you?"

Tori's eyes widened. "Like what?" she asked.

"When I started upstairs last night, I thought I saw a water bug fly by the end of the stairs," I whispered.

"Oh God," Tori shuddered. "I hate those things. Get roach traps when you're at the grocery store. Big ones."

"Don't worry," I said. "I plan to."

After I transferred my coffee to a paper cup, I started to walk out, but Tori stopped me. "Hey," she said, "hang on a sec."

She was staring at the mystery witch cup, which she'd taken down from the shelf over her work area.

"Yeah?" I said. "What's up?"

"Do you notice anything different about this cup?" she asked, holding it out to me.

I took the cup and turned it around, looking at it from all angles. "No," I said. "Why?"

"When you showed it to me yesterday, I could have sworn the witch was on the other side of the words," she replied.

You know how people say things like, "I don't know, I've slept since then?"

Well, sleeping would have been minor compared to everything that had happened to me since I found that cup.

"You're letting your imagination run away with you," I said.

"I guess," she said, still staring at the green-faced witch as she returned the cup to the shelf over the work area.

When I stepped out on the sidewalk, I heard a soft "meow" to my right. Festus was sprawled on the bench outside the cobbler shop.

"Good morning, you old rascal," I said.

With a wicked gleam in his eye, the cat answered, under his breath, "Don't I get my ears scratched?"

Before I could reply, Chase appeared in the doorway. "Dad," he muttered, "behave yourself." Looking over at me with hopeful eyes, he said hesitantly, "Hi."

When I smiled at him, those same eyes filled with so much relief, I felt my heart swell in my chest.

"Hi, yourself," I said. "Sorry for that abrupt exit last night."

"No problem," Chase said. "It was a lot for you to take in at one time."

That was one way of putting it.

"I was thinking we should all meet again tonight," I said. "Are you and . . . your cat . . . free?"

Festus regarded me impassively, yawned, and put his head down on his paws. "Very funny," he grumbled.

"We'll be there," Chase said. "And . . . could you and I . . . talk . . . later?"

"I'd like that," I said, "but I can tell you right now that what you're worried about is going to be okay. I'm not sure how yet, but we'll figure it out."

Chase regarded me curiously. "Has something happened?" he asked.

"A visit from the ancestors," I answered.

Anyone else would have looked at me like I'd lost my mind, but Chase smiled and nodded. "Good," he said. "The ones who came before us can generally see the path better than we can."

He sounded as if he spoke from experience, and I suddenly realized that it was going to be an incredible relief to talk this kind of thing over with someone who found it all perfectly normal.

"Okay," I said briskly. "We have a plan. Right now, I have doughnuts to buy and you need to get back to work."

Chase stood up straighter, as if at attention, and said, "Yes, ma'am."

Our easy exchange put even more of a spring in my step as I walked to the other end of the block. The grocery store was empty. Irma sat at her usual post on the stool at the cash register with her head buried in an "historical romance." This time the half-naked, chesty hunk on the cover was wearing a helmet with horns. Irma's reading tastes had apparently expanded to Vikings.

I filled one of the white paper bags with doughnuts and located the roach traps. Being careful to keep the two separate, I went up to the counter to pay. If Irma found the two purchases an odd combination, she didn't say so, probably because she was too focused on imparting the latest "news." Leaning toward me, she whispered breathlessly, "Have you heard?"

Irma loves to gossip. She missed her calling in life. The CIA could make good use of intelligence-gathering skills as sharp as hers.

"Heard what?" I asked, trying not to look amused.

"There's a new bakery or cooking shop or something like that going in over in the old hardware store," Irma said. "The lady who is running it is really sophisticated. She's definitely not from around here."

"Really?" I said, interested in spite of myself. "I wonder what made her decide to open her shop in Briar Hollow?"

As Irma rang up my purchase, she said, "Well, the ghost sightings are really helping the tourist trade this summer. I've already been talking to some of the other business people on the square about what we could do for Halloween. You know, it's almost as big as Christmas these days."

"Well, whatever you all come up with," I said, accepting my change, "count us in. What's this new woman's name?"

"I don't really remember her last name," Irma said, picking her book up again, "but her first name is Brenda."

That didn't raise any alarm bells with me until I stepped out of the shop and glanced over at the hardware store. The new owner was standing in the doorway and her name wasn't Brenda.

As I stared in shock, Brenna Sinclair smiled at me, raised her hand, and waved.

8

Earlier That Summer

Brenna Sinclair watched the scene in the cemetery from the wooded shadows beyond the rock wall. The newly raised spirits milled anxiously among the tombstones. The little witch who had released her from the coldness of the nether regions had also awakened them, but now she offered the ghosts no direction. Why would the child raise a spectral horde without a plan for its use?

Granted, Brenna herself animated shambling mobs during the Black Plague, but that was for her own amusement. The necromancy had been nothing more than the youthful indiscretion of a sorceress still shy of her 150th year. Terrorizing peasants grew old for her centuries ago. Brenna found the mortal rats roaming the halls of power to be far better sport. Morals decay with less stench and higher entertainment value.

The cemetery looked much as it had on that night of lightning and thunder when the Cherokee savage bound her in shackles worthy of Hephaestus himself. Brenna would have far preferred eternity in that lake of fire the religious scholars prattled about than the unendurable boredom of the nowhere from which she was now free.

The Druid, Duncan Skea, had been kinder than Knasgowa. He consigned Brenna to a sealed cavern in the Orkneys, but she had not known monotony there. Inside the cave, her magic continued to work. She used it to create comforts to stave off the madness of her isolation.

Her magic was her companion. Brenna held it close to her breast like a lover, allowing it to whisper deeper and deeper secrets in her ear. Then came the day when the light of insight pierced her understanding. She uttered the correct words and the seal on the stones broke.

On that day, Brenna stepped out on the windswept mountainside and drew in the clean, salty air off the ocean. With marks on the walls, she had tracked the passage of 108 years. Brenna was prepared to find a changed world. Instead, the islands' remoteness preserved her surroundings largely as she had known them on the day her son was born and stolen from her.

Brenna knew the men who were responsible for her exile were long dead, but she found her grandson, Angus, living in the Skea household. He spoke to her, offered her food and drink, but only as a ruse to give his son, Alexander, time to board a ship for the New World.

When Brenna realized what was happening, Angus tried to stop her, clutching in his hand a pathetic oak wand that Brenna snapped like a twig before she drove it through his traitorous heart. It was a pity, really. She had rather liked the man, but Brenna no longer had the luxury of trusting anyone who was not completely loyal to her.

Angus had not, however, died in vain, at least in terms of the success of his delaying tactic. Brenna arrived on the coast too late. Alexander's ship was already well out to sea.

Had she chosen, Brenna could have reached the deck on the wings of the wind, but that did not suit her purposes. Alexander was Brenna's only living descendant, a man of just 20 years. There was plenty of time to locate him and to encourage the young man to be more reasonable than his late father.

Let Alexander think he had escaped. Let him believe that any wilderness existed deep enough to shelter his presence. Rather than follow, Brenna sent only her voice on the morning breeze, whispering to Alexander the message that she would not be far behind his desperate flight.

The scent of fear on the night air drew Brenna's attention away from her memories. It was the young witch's apprehension she tasted. How could this mere child have undone Knasgowa's magic, yet seem so terrified now? What game was she playing?

Brenna cautiously extended her senses, careful not to betray her presence. The girl felt impossibly young, and her roiling emotions tasted so very sweet. She should be easily corruptible. Brenna did not know in what year she now found herself, but the energy of the world was far different than she remembered.

On her last night in this reality she had been a sorceress for almost 770 years. The eighteen years that came before that counted for nothing but a dim memory of misery and subservience. No matter what befell her, Brenna would never allow herself to be so weak again. Her days as a victim ended the night she entered the blackest reaches of the forest and traded her mortality for real power.

"Sure be thee of this path, mortal?" the wizened hag cackled. "Thee asks to die to all thee has known. Thy path never again will return to where thee now stand. No children will comfort thy bones that will never age. Want this, do thee?"

Brenna wanted it. The hot blood of revenge coursed through the veins of the woman who walked out of those woods to maim and torture the callous men who treated her as their chattel.

From that night forward her choices were her own -- until Hamish Crawford was cast upon the beach below her remote Orkney home.

Immortality demands the periodic ruse. Brenna went to the Orkney Islands to disappear briefly, to allow the mortals to forget that business in Paris. The court of King Louis XIV had been so charmingly amusing until Madame de Brinvilliers and her lover, Captain Godin de Sainte-Croix, began poisoning men.

The good Captain conveniently died before he could be charged, but, of course, with a woman accused of perpetrating three murders -- her father and both of her brothers -- the behavior was attributed to witchcraft. And just as inconveniently for Brenna, she had been friendly with the cursed woman.

While the remote Orkneys were a bit of an extreme choice, Brenna had wanted time alone to pick her next venue from among the courts of Europe. She could watch the political currents in the polished depths of her looking glass, study the ebb and tide of power, and enter the game again at a time and place of her choosing.

But then a wretched man of religious principle washed ashore on her beach. Brenna had no idea why she took Hamish in, why she nursed him to health, or why she let herself feel love for him. The physical pleasures of his company were no better or worse than those she had known from any of the men with whom she had toyed, but there was that fire of conviction in Hamish she found compelling.

Then she became pregnant, the very thing the old crone had told her could never happen, and suddenly Brenna's concept of power evolved. The Hereditarium witches, the ones born with their abilities, looked down on her kind, refused alliances with the Creavit that would have ended the dominion of the puny mortals on earth.

But what if Brenna could found her own dynasty? One that

would control not just the mortals, but put an end to the restraining hand of the Hereditarium? Then the world would be hers for the taking.

In whatever year Brenna now found herself, she knew traces of her own blood must still exist. Knasgowa interrupted the plan; she hadn't succeeded in stopping it.

As Brenna watched, the witch in the cemetery conferred with the shade of the man in uniform. The other girl, the one with the flaming highlights in her blond hair, appeared to be a close associate. Perhaps a member of the witch's coven? The blond girl felt oddly familiar to Brenna, but she could not understand why.

A sound made Brenna look skyward. A massive flying creature crossed the blanket of stars, lights blinking at the tips of its rigid wings. Had she awakened in a time when giants once again roamed the earth? But she felt no magic from the flyer, no life. Had humans advanced to the point of building flying machines?

The thought made Brenna smile. Her mind returned to an evening drinking wine with an artist. What was his name? Something Da Vinci? He'd shown her sketches of a flying machine. When was that? The 1400s? So like mortals. Slow. Stinted. Grasping innovation at the speed of the inconsequential little snails they were. But if the human world was more developed than it had been in 1853 that might well work to Brenna's advantage.

Turning back to the cemetery, she saw the two women and the gray specter preparing to leave in the company of the insufferable little brownie Alexander had brought with him from the Orkneys. Some people harbor such affection for their pets. Before Brenna was done, she would be sure to put an end to that creature's obsequious interferences.

Brenna moved swiftly along the wall to keep the group in sight. As she watched, they climbed into some type of conveyance that moved silently under its own power. Brenna muttered soft words, rising from the ground and fading from sight to glide unseen above the strange horseless carriage.

When the vehicle reached the center of town, Brenna drew back. She recognized the square, or at least one building on the north side. Flameless lights on poles cast pale illumination over the scene. The carriage pulled behind the buildings. After a moment or two, Brenna saw a light in one of the store windows. That was when she felt it. The power of the aos sí.

"So," she whispered, a slow smile spreading over her face, "the battlefield is made anew, but the enemy remains the same."

Brenna knew where she was; now it was time to find out when.

Only one other light burned on the square. The establishment appeared to be some type of eatery. Brenna could see a man sitting at a table, papers spread out around him. Periodically, he tapped his fingers on a box sitting to his right before making marks on the papers with a pencil.

Silently, Brenna crossed the square and knocked on the glass inset in the door. The man looked up, startled. He pushed back his chair and walked toward her. "Uh, hi," he said, "we're, uh, closed."

"Forgive me for disturbing you," Brenna said, fixing him with her stare. She barely finished the mesmer spell before his eyes glazed over.

"That's . . . I mean . . . it's not a problem," the man stammered.

"Let me in," Brenna commanded softly.

The man unlocked the door and Brenna stepped into the building.

"What year is this?" she asked.

"It's 2015," the man said, his voice distant and compliant.

So, they'd kept her imprisoned for 162 years this time.

"Sit down," Brenna told the man, "and tell me of this world. What is your name?"

"Pete," the man said, walking back to the table and pulling out a chair for her.

Manners. That would work in his favor. Brenna sat down, pointing for Pete to join her. When he did, she asked, "What is this device?"

"It's a laptop," he answered.

"What does it do?"

"Uh, stuff," he said lamely, "like email and getting on the Internet."

"What is this Internet?"

"It's . . . well . . . it's where all the information is," Pete said hesitantly.

"You mean a library?" Brenna asked.

"Sort of," Pete replied. "Nobody really knows how it works. We just use it."

Brenna smiled at him, turning up the full force of her personality. She enjoyed the flush that spread over his cheeks and the look of hopeful pleasure filling his eyes.

"How fascinating, Peter," she said, turning her voice into a silken purr. "Show me. Show me everything."

By the time the first rays of the rising sun slanted across the square, Brenna already understood the potential of the 21st century. With her powers and abilities this could be a most interesting time for her. Better even than the Renaissance, or the Reformation when it had been so ridiculously easy to leverage self-righteous men of faith to do as she pleased.

That peasant monk? Luther? The one who was given credit for starting the upheaval that served her and her kind so well? He had been even easier to manipulate than this man Peter who made his living covering circles of dough with tomato sauce.

Pizza, he called it, a vile Neopolitan creation according to the Internet.

Pete was in the front room now, preparing to serve the tedious fare to the general public at what he referred to as the "lunch run."

Brenna was comfortably ensconced in his living quarters. At least the insufferable fool had a decent supply of wine. She'd given him a list of items to procure for her, but had been gracious enough to allow him the time to attend to his business. There was no need in calling attention to the establishment, which was the only eatery on the square.

Pete gratefully assured her that he often closed for the afternoon, and would promptly get her everything she needed as soon as his last customer left.

Brenna was too busy to deal with the man at the moment anyway. She found the Internet both fascinating and ridiculously infantile, especially a location called "Facebook," an apparent monument to the narcissistic tendencies of humans. From it, however, she was gaining an excellent education in the prejudices, fears and foibles of the modern masses.

When the stream of information had suddenly shut down earlier in the day, Pete babbled some gibberish about his "bandwidth" problems. Brenna dismissed him with a wave of her hand that also served to open the channel of data like a gushing torrent.

The pathetic little box was incapable of handling it all, so now Brenna was surrounded by additional screens conjured with a wave of her hand. They floated suspended in the air around her. The Internet was proving to be far more useful than the looking glass that had once been her window on the world.

Brenna had long since abandoned the ridiculous convention of the "keyboard." She had no time for mechanical hurdles. Magic freed her to follow multiple avenues of inquiry spontaneously, to make connections and isolate items of particular interest, including the present location of her funds.

Throughout the centuries, Brenna had made it her business to cultivate friendships with the greatest bankers. The Medici, Rothschilds, Welsers, Fuggers, Gosslers - she had known them all. The bulk of her life had been lived in times when the suspicion of witchcraft was a stain best avoided. In order to manipulate the affairs of men to her advantage, Brenna acquired the things they valued in ways they respected. Nothing spoke more powerfully than money.

With meticulous care, Brenna created a modern identity for herself, and gained access to her long dormant, but highly secure accounts by posing as her own descendant. When a hurdle presented itself, she used a mixture of magic and technology to solve the problem and move on.

When she was satisfied that she "existed" at a level sufficient to move about freely in the mortal world, Brenna turned her attention to the next most pressing matter. Who was the witch from the cemetery and how had she come to be aligned with the aos sí?

9

I'd like to tell you my response to seeing Brenna was epic, that I did something to earn my broomstick, but honestly? Before I realized what I was doing, I waved back.

Before you land all over me, admit it. Some things are just programmed in us. Saying "bless you" for a sneeze, answering "fine" to "how are you," and waving back.

Trust me. The instant I did it, I felt like an idiot. Especially since Brenna gave me a smile that assured me she thought I *was* an idiot.

The answering wave seemed to tell her all she needed or wanted to know, because she stepped back inside and closed the door. My disoriented brain stopped talking to my feet while it processed a wave of did-that-just-happen confusion.

Irma's voice snapped me back to reality. "Jinx, honey? Did you forget something?"

"No, ma'am," I stammered.

(Also an autopilot response in the south.)

My legs finally picked up a wobbly nerve impulse and I moved, forcing myself not to run. That's how desperate I felt to get back to the store and Myrtle's protection. Thankfully Festus was no longer on the bench by the front door of the cobbler's shop. I wasn't about to try to explain what had just happened to anyone but Tori until I had some time to process the incident.

The instant I made it through the front door, Tori abandoned her post and came out from behind the espresso to meet me in the middle of the store.

"Are you okay?" she asked quietly but urgently, putting her hand on my arm. "You look like you've seen a ghost." Then she lowered her voice even more. "Oh my God. *Did* you see a ghost? I mean one we don't already know?"

Shaking my head, I said, "Storeroom. Now."

Tori turned toward the handful of customers seated at the tables. "Hey, guys," she called out cheerfully, "we'll be in the storeroom. Ring the bell if you need anything."

There were a few raised-hand replies, but most of our patrons didn't even look up from their books or tablets.

As soon as we were out of earshot, I told Tori what had happened. To my considerable consternation, her immediate reply to my bombshell was, "Are you sure it was Brenna?"

"Oh my God, Tori, *seriously*?" I said, adrenaline still pumping through my veins. "You did *not* just ask me that question! Of course I'm sure it's her! I'm telling you, Brenna Sinclair is right over there in the old hardware store this very minute."

Even saying the words scared me more than I was willing to think about, but something else had begun to stir in the back of my mind. Through the buzz of incoherence, a voice was asking, "*Why* didn't you go over there and ask her what the *hell* she's doing in your town?"

That voice was a sign of things to come, and a huge leap from where I had been a few hours earlier -- gasping for air on the side of a country road in the middle of a panic attack.

A girl can change a lot in a few hours when circumstances demand it.

Believe me. I was definitely experiencing a period of high demand.

Tori's next question surprised me.

"How does she look?"

Huh. Not what I was expecting, which may well have been what Tori intended, since to give her an answer, I had to stop and think. That slight pause let me get some of my focus back.

"Um, she looks kinda fantastic," I admitted. "High-end clothes, great hair. Not like someone who got fried with blue lightning."

"How is that even possible?" Tori said. "I mean, we tossed the bucket of water on her. We sang 'ding dong the witch is dead.' That should have been game over."

Until that moment, I viewed our confrontation with Brenna in the cemetery as a win for our side, too. Which I guess it was, since she left and all of the spirits I accidentally raised went back to their graves. But, if I broke that night down frame by frame, there was no proof we'd done anything except make Brenna disappear.

Tori saw the realization on my face. "Uh-oh," she said. "What?"

"We shouldn't have thought it was game over," I answered. "All we can really say for sure is that we put on a heck of a light show. We assumed we killed her, or banished her, or *something*. We don't know that we did any of that."

Tori looked at me with a stunned expression. "And you're just *now* thinking about this?" she asked incredulously. "Late to the party, much?"

"Hey!" I protested. "You didn't think about it either. You were as happy as I was to believe we'd seen the last of her. But you have to admit, the whole thing was a little too easy."

That won me Tori's signature cocked eyebrow. "Easy? Like

the part where I sliced open the palm of my hand with a dagger?" she asked. "Thus creating *blood*?"

"And that would be the same dagger that sliced *my* arm open," I countered. "Thus creating *more* blood."

We are competitive in all things, including knife fights.

Honestly, neither of us had more than thin, pale scars to show for getting cut, but there had, indeed, been blood. In fact, it was the blood that saved us and opened up new potential avenues not just for my power, but for abilities that Tori and I might share. There had been a couple of kinda spooky, kinda cool mind reading moments in the last few weeks.

Myrtle speculated that if we worked at it, Tori and I might master the skill. It was on the "To Do List," but the list kept getting longer by the minute.

"Okay," Tori said, "so we drew the wrong conclusions from that night. Our bad. Moving on. The major point here is that you *saw* Brenna. Did she actually do anything or did she just stand there?"

An involuntary shudder moved through me. "That was the creepy part," I said. "She waved at me."

Both of Tori's eyebrows shot up. "She *waved* at you?" she asked. "Are we talking an insincere-stuck-up-girl wave or a menacing I'm-ending-you-come-sundown wave?"

I held my hand up and rocked it back and forth at the wrist. "That kind of wave," I replied.

Tori frowned. "Well, that's not very evil-sorceress-raised-from-the-dead," she said, sounding disappointed.

"Tori!" I exclaimed in frustration. "What are you? The Russian judge who never gives a 10? Would you be happier if Brenna had hurled a fireball at me?"

"You have to admit that would have been more in character," Tori pointed out.

Which was true.

I glanced over my shoulder to double check no one could overhear us, and then hissed, "Myrtle! Are you listening to this?"

Somewhere in the air above our heads, we heard the three-note trill Myrtle uses to signal agreement. She only appears to us in human form when we're down in the basement. Up top in the store, she relies on a creative language of sound effects and sight gags to get her point across.

"How the *heck* did Brenna manage to set up shop right here on the courthouse square without you knowing about it?" I demanded. "You picked a great time to start sleeping on the job."

After a few seconds, Rodney emerged from the liniment cans that hide his bachelor pad from view. (We don't like to use the word "cage." Rodney is very much a free agent.) He was running on three legs, holding a tiny parchment scroll in one front paw.

As we watched, the rat jumped from his shelf to the top of the filing cabinet and held the roll of paper out to me.

"Thank you, Rodney," I said, taking the message. Untying the satin ribbon, I pulled the parchment flat and found an answer to my question, penned in Myrtle's neat, precise hand. I read it aloud.

"For the record, I do not require sleep, and I did not know Brenna was close by because she does not register on what you would call my 'radar.' I believe the status of her powers has changed. We'll talk about it tonight. For right now, don't sweat it."

I looked up incredulously. "Don't *sweat* it?"

Rodney cocked his head as if listening, retraced his steps, and returned with a second scroll.

This one said, "Lighten up, dear."

"Okay, fine," I grumbled, "but will you at least tell me if you think 'changed status' means her powers are gone?"

The three-note trill sounded again.

Tori held out her arm to Rodney, who accepted the invitation to position himself on her shoulder. "We're gonna have to get you a Western Union uniform like in the old movies, little guy," she crooned, stroking the silky fur between his ears. Rodney nodded his head eagerly.

Looking over at me, Tori said, "Come on, we're letting perfectly good doughnuts go uneaten."

That elicited more eager head nodding from Rodney. Aunt Fiona let him eat whatever he wanted when she was alive, but I insist on one meal of certified, fortified rodent chow per day. Rodney, like Tori, lives for junk food. He eats the pellets, but he doesn't love them. Doughnuts he loves.

Tori took the white sack from me while I put the roach traps on a nearby shelf.

Gesturing toward my favorite, battered armchair, Tori said, "Sit. I'll get fresh coffee for us."

Since the health department would not have appreciated her walking around the shop with a black-and-white rat on her shoulder, Tori transferred Rodney to me before she left. He slipped under the collar of my shirt and snuggled against my neck, which was both a sign of affection and optimal placement for doughnut pilferage.

Tori came back bearing two huge mugs of something hot and caffeinated.

"Why didn't you use the new witch mug?" I asked, taking the cup she held out to me.

"Because it gives me the creeps, that's why," Tori said. "I still think that witch moved."

Snagging a jelly doughnut from the sack, I said, "Well, if she did, she's all of three inches tall, so I think we can take her. Now, spill. What happened after I left last night?"

Tori bit into a chocolate-covered doughnut, chewed for a minute, and then said nonchalantly, "Oh, not much. Myrtle just told me I'm next in line to be head Alchemist up in The Valley."

I swear to you, she waited until I was swallowing to drop that little bombshell. I coughed so hard, Tori had to lean over and pound my back. Rodney hung on for dear life until I could sit up straight again.

"Hey," she ordered, "no choking. I'm not in the mood to do the Heimlich and you're upsetting Rodney."

When I could finally breathe, I apologized to the rat, slipped him a piece of jelly doughnut, and demanded to know if Tori was pulling my leg. It wouldn't have been the first time she came out with something outrageous just to enjoy my reaction.

"Nope," she said. "It was a total 'into every generation is born' moment. Seems like the scrying test was more than just to find out if I was evil. The amulet was an alchemical Breathalyzer. I blew over the magical limit."

"And that means what?"

A wide grin split her face. "It means we're going to The Valley to meet the wizard."

"Alchemist," I corrected.

"Uh, no," Tori said. "We're actually going to meet the wizard first. Barnaby Shevington is still Lord High Mayor."

My jaw dropped. "But wouldn't that make him ancient?"

"About 475 years ancient," Tori said, snagging another doughnut. "Myrtle spent a lot of time trying to explain the whole time thing to me including talking about the moms. They kinda left some stuff out, Jinksy."

"Well," I said, "they did say they wanted Myrtle to tell us the rest of the story. What's the gist of it?"

"The whole part about them not being powerful wasn't really true," Tori said. "You know how Myrtle and Fiona keep telling you that you're the strongest witch in generations? Well, they thought that about Kelly, too, but then the thing with the cheerleaders happened and she and my Mom bailed on them."

"Taking us with them," I said slowly.

"Exactly," Tori said, "but from what I can tell, when we accidentally figured out how to combine our blood at the cemetery, we proved we can handle this mega 'blood magic' stuff that makes us the real deal they've been looking for."

"To do what?" I asked.

"Myrtle was kind of vague on that," she said, "but she did tell me I'm supposed to be the next alchemist and she wants you to meet Barnaby Shevington."

"Tell me again how this guy is still alive?" I asked.

"According to Myrtle," Tori said, "time in The Valley moves slower, so the people who live there don't age at the same rate we do."

"So what happens to us when we go there?" I asked.

"The rules of their time stream apply to us."

Well, that was better than Botox.

With the way the morning was turning out, a second doughnut seemed more than in order. After I gave Rodney a bite, I leaned back in my chair and looked at Tori speculatively. "You know none of this can be a coincidence, right?"

"You mean Brenna showing up potentially powerless right after we find out there's a door to a hidden magical valley in our basement and we're both part of some kind of witch dynasty?" she said.

As usual, we were on the same page.

"So what do you think she's up to?" I asked.

"I have no idea," Tori said, "but I agree with Myrtle. Brenna is just letting us know she's here. If she wanted to torch our butts with a ball of fire or storm the basement door, she would have done it already. That is if she's even able to do it."

Since we hadn't seen anything to suggest that anger management was Brenna's forte, that made me feel a lot better, as did the idea that she was no longer an evil sorceress but just a plain ordinary evil human.

"Okay," I conceded, "so that explains why she's out there in plain sight. She knows we're not going to do anything to her with the whole town square watching us."

"Right," Tori said. "Powers or no powers, I think she's playing some kind of long game."

It was my turn to frown. "What do you know about playing the long game?" I asked. "For that matter, what *is* a long game?"

"Myrtle is teaching me to play chess," Tori said, grinning. "A long game is when you're thinking a whole lot of moves in advance of what you just did. You give up a piece and it looks stupid, but you have a bigger goal in mind three moves down the road."

Don't ever underestimate Tori. My girl is smart. She is gonna rock the whole Alchemist thing.

"So you're saying Brenna just wanted to rattle me," I said.

"And behold her success," Tori replied.

I eyed her suspiciously. "What's with all this Zen calm? Have I missed something?"

Tori grinned. "Uh, yeah," she said. "In case you haven't noticed, we are moving up fast in the bad-ass witch club ourselves. All I've got to say to Brenna is, 'Bring it.'"

Which made me remember I hadn't told Tori about my vision of the coven yet. When I finished describing the women to her and repeated what Johanna said, I was surprised to see Tori's eyes shining with tears.

"Doesn't that make you incredibly proud, Jinksy?" she asked. "I mean, we're part of this whole awesome legacy. *Us.* Can you just imagine all the things those women must have done in their lives? Everything they achieved and overcame. Doesn't it make you want to know them?"

Trust me, if I could have crawled straight into my vision and sat with Johanna, Myrtle, and the coven, I would have. Of course, I wanted to know them.

"The awesomeness is why I'm not as freaked out as I was last night," I said. "Even with finding out Brenna is back, I'm feeling a lot better."

"Does that include lack of freakage about Chase?" Tori asked gently. "'Cause I really think he's one of the good guys."

I nodded, coloring a little. "I know," I said. "I saw him out front when I was on my way to get the doughnuts. I told him it was going to be okay. I don't know how, but it is."

Tori flashed me a wicked and thoroughly approving grin. "Well, girl," she said, "he is one seriously hot tomcat."

Heat rushed to my face. "Stop!" I ordered. "You're as bad as Festus."

"Not even close," Tori said. "I killed half a bottle of Scotch with that scoundrel after the meeting broke up last night. He can tell stories that would put a preacher in his grave."

"I have no doubt," I said. "This morning he wanted to know if I was going to scratch his ears."

Tori snickered. "He likes belly rubs, too."

"*STOP!*"

She laughed out loud at that, and I swear to you, Rodney giggled.

"So, while we're doing the whole disclosure thing," she said, "Amity is a witch."

Of course she is.

What the heck, I snagged the third doughnut.

Tori explained about Amity's entrance following my exit and how she had remained undercover during the Brenna incident on orders from Myrtle.

"Since you've got the freaking-out thing under control," Tori said, "I thought I better give you the heads up that Amity will be there tonight."

"I appreciate that," I said, and then something occurred to

me. "How do Amity and Chase get into the basement anyway?" I
asked curiously.

"Their basement doors open to the same dimension," Tori
said, which touched off another round of explanations.

It made sense that the basement was part of the place "in
between." There was no other way to reconcile the size of the
space in relation to the footprint of the store.

"You found out about *all* of this after I left last night?" I asked.
"Was I gone that long?"

"If you want to keep up with the class, Jinksy, you better can
the dramatic exits," Tori advised. "We're in Honors Metaphysics
these days. No cutting out."

Since I had apparently missed Time Theory 101, Name That
Alchemist, and a drinking game with an alley cat, it was good
advice.

"So did Myrtle say what happens next?" I asked.

Tori shook her head. "She said we need to go up to The
Valley, but that we had to wait for you to get on board. Which
I'm guessing you are now."

I was onboard all right. No more letting someone else drive
my train.

10

For the rest of the day, I continued to follow Beau's advice. I did normal things. That didn't stop me from stealing glances at the clock, but I did manage to stay sufficiently occupied so that I didn't jump out of my skin every time the bell on the front door jingled.

I won't try to convince you that I didn't think about Brenna, but I didn't obsess about her. Sometimes the greatest power a person has over you is their ability to get inside your head. If nothing else, I could deprive Brenna of that victory.

Unfortunately, that wasn't the only deprivation I caused that day. At least half a dozen times during the afternoon, I glanced out the window only to find Chase watching me, while pretending *not* to watch me. He always managed to disguise the watching -- talking to someone on the street, pretending to study the newspaper in his hand -- but he *was* watching.

I don't mean to imply he was going all creepy stalker boy on me. I knew he wanted to have a conversation. *I* wanted to have the conversation. But there was just too much going on. "Too much" being the operative phrase. Too confused. Too over-whelmed. Too busy trying to put the pieces together. He had to make do with a smile and a wave. It was really all I had to give him at the moment, but I hated having him standing out there feeling on the edge of uncertainty all the same.

It helped that the espresso bar stayed full all day. At some point in the afternoon, as I was going back and forth dusting shelves, I realized we had suddenly acquired several chess sets. Two of our patrons were bent over game pieces dressed as Union and Confederate soldiers, while another pair waged a strategic battle between the University of North Carolina Tarheels and the Duke Blue Devils.

A third board sat off to one side untouched. The pieces were hand carved bits of musical notation. The bass clef king towered over the treble clef queen. Quarter notes stood by as bishops next to quarter rest knights and sharp rooks. A row of eighth-note pawns guarded the front line for each side.

Piano lessons. Four years.

Intrigued, I bent closer and looked at the designated columns. Instead of the alphabet, I found the labels C, D, E, F, G, A, B, C. It took me a minute to realize what I was seeing. The notation on this board was based on the C-major scale. Very clever. And apparently overwhelming for our clientele, since no one had approached the beautifully crafted little battleground.

The next time I went behind the counter, I said to Tori, "Great picks on the chessboards."

She looked up from drying a tray of cups. "I thought you bought those," she said.

"No," I replied, "I didn't. I used to play a little bit with my dad, but not in years. It hadn't even occurred to me that chess sets might go over big with the customers. That musical board is gorgeous, by the way."

"Huh," Tori said, staring out over the tables. "Maybe it's Myrtle's doing since she's teaching me to play. And, yes, the musical board is beautiful, but it's the funniest thing. When I came out this morning, all the major pieces were on the table pushed over to one side. There were just a few pawns on the board itself."

"You mean like someone had been playing?" I asked.

She shook her head. "No," she said, "the way the pawns were arranged couldn't have been from play. They were all lined up in columns. That doesn't happen in a game."

Before we could talk about the mysterious chess sets, two of our older customers, who were already coming in every afternoon regular as clockwork, got into an argument over the legality of a move.

As we watched them bicker, I said to Tori, "We have to put in a regular coffee pot."

"Why?" she asked.

"Because if we're going to be giving free refills, they'll break us on the good stuff," I answered. Just then, the man wearing the John Deere tractor cap snatched it off and smacked his opponent over the head.

"You boys play nice," I commanded in my best authoritarian waitress voice.

They both shot me sheepish looks and resumed their argument at a quieter and less physical level.

Tori laughed. "I see your point," she said. "I'll order one tonight, and a good supply of some normal, cheap, highly caffeinated coffee."

There were no more chess-related confrontations for the remainder of the afternoon, but in addition to the old men camped at their game boards, we had a steady stream of customers. When 5:30 rolled around, I had to gently, but firmly kick the last of our newfound regulars out. They were good-natured about the eviction, promising to see me tomorrow.

I made a mental note to go down to the corner the next morning and buy several newspapers to leave out on the counter

-- and some sharpened pencils in case some of the guys liked to work the crossword puzzle or that Sudoku thing that makes absolutely no sense to me.

My mental shopping list brought a smile to my face. We were creating a truly enjoyable atmosphere in the store, one of our own making, not something inherited from Aunt Fiona. The sense of accomplishment felt good, and it represented something blessedly normal. The very thing Beau Longworth told me I needed. He was right.

"What time did you tell Myrtle we'd be downstairs?" I asked Tori as she wiped off the counter in the espresso bar.

"She said to just come down when we were ready," Tori answered, draping the towel over the edge of the sink to dry, "but I think we better have something to eat first. Lord only knows what's in store for us this evening. Come on. I've got some tuna fish and rye at my place. I'll make sandwiches."

"Cool," I said. "I'm just gonna run upstairs and feed the cats."

Fifteen minutes later, when I tapped on Tori's door, she was setting our plates, a bowl of chips, and two sodas on the table. "How's the herd?" she asked.

"The usual," I said. "Yule tried to dig to China in the litter box again. Winston left a hairball in the middle of the living room rug. Zeke was sound asleep on his back in the windowsill. And Xavier destroyed another roll of toilet paper."

"Ah," she said, "life with cats. Maybe you can get Chase to reason with them."

It hadn't even occurred to me that Chase probably could talk to my cats in felinese. Or maybe he already had and that was why the cats loved him so much.

"I'm not sure that's a conversation I want to initiate," I said, pulling out one of the chairs and sitting down. "Those furry felons know too much about me." Then, almost as an afterthought, I said, "Have you seen Darby today?"

"Not since I asked him to tell Myrtle you wanted everyone to get together again tonight," she said, joining me. "He was so excited, he popped out of sight without a word. Then he popped back in to give me Myrtle's answer. I haven't seen him since."

It wasn't long before we learned why our resident brownie was so charged up. As soon as we finished eating, we walked downstairs and found everyone waiting for us with backpacks and walking sticks no less. I was amused to see that Festus was sitting on top of what must have been Chase's bag, half dozing inside a mesh compartment apparently designed for his riding comfort.

I looked at Amity, who was stuffing a sketchbook and pencil case in the front pocket of her pack, and said, without preamble, "You could have told me, you know. It would have made things a whole lot easier."

She smiled and shrugged. "That's what I said, but Myrtle and Fiona had other ideas."

Gesturing towards the pile of gear, I asked, "What's with all this stuff?"

Darby's hand shot up. Most of the time he dressed like a garden gnome but without the pointed cap. Today he was wearing lederhosen and an alpine hat. When I nodded for him to go ahead and answer my question, the little guy bobbed up and down with so much enthusiasm, I was afraid the flapping of the plumed feather in his hat band would lift him straight off the ground.

"We are going to The Valley, Mistress," he said, breathlessly. "I am going to see my friends for the first time since Master Alexander asked me to guard Mistress Knasgowa's grave."

Well, that explained his fancy dress.

Taking in the extent of the luggage, Tori said, "Uh, exactly how long is this visit supposed to last?"

Myrtle, who was perusing the bookshelves to the left of the

fireplace, pulled a volume off the shelf and said brusquely, "A few days."

When she saw the stunned look on our faces, she added, "Don't worry, I had Darby pack your things. If everyone is ready, we should be leaving."

Without so much as a word, the others started picking up their packs, only to pause uncertainly when I said in a firm voice, "Hold the phone."

I meant what I said about that business of driving my own train, and this was the perfect time for everyone else to get that message loud and clear.

Myrtle regarded me with a perplexed expression. "Is there a problem?"

"Yes, there is," I said. "First off, none of you bothered to ask *me* about this excursion. Second, what about the store? And my cats? I can't just pick up and be gone several days without warning, never mind that we really need to talk about the fact that *Brenna Sinclair* has set up shop on the square."

When Myrtle drew down the corners of her mouth and seemed prepared to lecture me, Chase hastily jumped in.

"In this time stream we'll be back before morning," he assured me. "There's too much to see in The Valley to just come and go in a few hours. You'll like it, Jinx." He paused, and then added, "I'd like to show it to you."

Aw, man! *So* not fair. Here I was prepared to dig my heels in and set my own metaphysical schedule, and I had a good-looking man offering to show me the sights in a secluded, magical valley. How the heck was I supposed to say no to that?

I made a show of thinking about the invitation. The rest of the group shifted uneasily, and Myrtle fixed me with a thoroughly disapproving gaze. Festus, however, wasn't buying it. I heard him make that hacking pre-hairball cough I knew only too well, interspersed with the words "mush" and "nonsense."

Shooting the old tomcat a warning glare, and making a mental note to ask if we could have two clocks in the basement -- one set to Valley time -- I relented on all points but one.

"I'm not going anywhere until we talk about Brenna," I said finally.

"There will be plenty of time to talk about that woman," Myrtle replied dismissively.

"There's no time like the present," I responded with stubborn sweetness.

Sighing, Myrtle said in a long-suffering tone, "I see you are determined to embrace the less than admirable tradition of obstinacy cherished by the women in your family."

I just looked at her.

She had no idea how much I could "cherish the obstinacy."

Several heartbeats passed, and then she let out another massive sigh.

It didn't work.

Ancient Fae or not, she could stand right in front of me and hyperventilate for all I cared. I wasn't budging.

I'm won't say Myrtle caved exactly, but she did finally meet me halfway.

"Very well," she said, her tone dripping resignation. "Brenna is putting out no more signal than the other humans on the square. Because of that, I don't think she's an immediate threat, but I want to discuss the matter with Moira, which is one of the reasons we need to be on our way. Are you satisfied?"

No, I wasn't satisfied. She answered one question and raised 20 more, but I wasn't ready to get in a real contest of wills with the aos sí and find myself turned into a toadstool or something. I confined my follow-up questions to two.

"What do you mean by 'signal' and who is Moira?"

"Oh, for heaven sake's," Myrtle said impatiently, "we really do not have time for a classroom lecture!"

Maybe she didn't have time, but I certainly did.

And what the heck was wrong with her anyway? Myrtle was never this testy.

Again, I stood and waited.

Finally, Myrtle said, "All living beings generate an energy signal. When I choose to do so, I can hear the background hum of humanity. Those with magical powers stand out for me. Other than the people in this room, there are no other magical beings within the range of my perceptions. Brenna has either lost her powers or she is masking them in some way. *Now* are you satisfied?"

I didn't like the sound of the whole masked powers thing. "On the off chance that she does still have her powers, should we be leaving the store unguarded?" I asked.

Amity fielded that one. "The store is warded," she said. "I cast the spell myself. Nothing can happen here that we won't know about in The Valley."

Okay. Magical LoJack. That was good.

"And this Moira person?" I asked, still standing my ground. "Who is she?"

"She is the Alchemist," Myrtle answered. "If Tori is to be apprenticed by her, they must meet as soon as possible. And Barnaby is quite anxious to speak with you. Neither of those things can happen as long as we are standing here wasting time."

I looked at Tori. I could tell from the expression in her eyes that she was almost as excited as Darby but was trying to be *way* more cool about it.

"You up for this?" I asked.

It was a completely unnecessary question.

"Kick the tires and light the fires, baby," she grinned.

Great. *Top Gun* quotes. Just what I needed. Tori in Maverick mode.

"Okay," I said. "Which pack is mine?"

Darby looked so happy and relieved I thought he might cry. "I selected the red one for you, Mistress, and the yellow is for Tori," he said.

Our favorite colors.

It is impossible not to love Darby. They should put a picture of him beside the word "thoughtful" in the dictionary.

I tested the weight of the pack, then slipped the straps over my shoulders and took the walking staff Amity held out to me. The polished oak felt instantly familiar to my hand, and as soon as I touched the wood, the chunk of raw quartz set in the top of the staff began to pulsate slightly.

"She likes you," Amity said approvingly.

"She?" I asked, watching the stone with open fascination.

"The staff was a gift to Knasgowa from the ancient oak that stands in the center of The Village Green in Shevington," Amity explained. "Your ancestors have carried this staff with them on their trips to The Valley for more than 200 years."

I ran my fingers over the wood and felt ... life.

"Does she have a name?" I asked.

Myrtle answered, the tone of her voice now filled with affection. "She is called Dílestos. In the ancient language of the Celts it means to be steadfast and loyal. The tree in the center of Shevington sprang from the roots of the great oak under which I made my home in the time before there was time. Learn to hear her voice, Jinx, and she will guide you well."

"Dílestos," I whispered, opening my mind to the staff. "Hi there."

The last time I communicated with a tree, I'd placed my hands on the trunk of an aged, venerable hickory and found myself drawn into its alien awareness of time and space. Dílestos was different. More refined and purposeful. More *present*.

Then, I hadn't learned about the Celtic perception of the oak tree as a storehouse of knowledge. I didn't know Druids used oak staffs to access other facets of reality, like the one we were about to visit. But I did feel the weight of the oak's constancy, and when a single word, warm as a summer wind, flowed through my mind, I smiled.

Dílestos said, "Friend."

I felt Tori's eyes on me and looked up.

"Hey," she said, "what's going on over there?"

"It's like that night," I answered softly, "when the hickory spoke to me."

Myrtle said quietly, "You are learning to find the life in all things. Remember, Jinx, the blood of the Cherokee people flows in your veins. Your connection with this land is far deeper than you realize."

Tori turned to Myrtle. "Wasn't Duncan Skea a Druid?" she asked.

Myrtle nodded. "Yes," she said, "he was."

"So, I have Druid blood, too," Tori said, "and the Druids were big on trees, right?"

"Correct," Myrtle said, a smile tugging at the corners of her mouth.

"So does that mean I can learn to talk to trees?" Tori went on.

"Yes," Myrtle said, "the trees are our sisters and brothers. They draw their wisdom from the deep memories of the earth. When you discover that part of yourself that stems from your Druidic ancestors, you will hear their voices just as Jinx can."

Since the theme of the evening seemed to be discovery, I didn't see any reason why Tori had to wait. I held Dílestos out to her.

"Go on," I said. "Try it."

She hesitated for just an instant. "Okay," she said, tentatively reaching for the staff, "but don't let go."

"I won't," I said. "I promise."

Tori laid her hand next to mine on Dílestos. The pulsations

of the stone changed their rhythm and a faint blue glow stirred in the facets of the quartz.

After a couple of seconds, Tori's eyes grew round in her face. "What is it?" I asked.

"She said 'Welcome,'" Tori said, grinning in disbelief. "I heard her say 'Welcome.'"

"Excellent!" Amity said. "She likes you both. That's even better than we had hoped."

I remember exactly what ran through my mind when she said that.

Why the heck does it always feel like we're being asked to pass tests we don't even know we're taking?

The instant I thought the words, Dílestos whispered, "Get used to it."

In spite of myself, I laughed.

"What?" Tori asked curiously.

"I'll explain it later," I said. "Let's just say Dílestos is our kind of gal."

Upstairs in the store

In the darkened area behind the espresso bar, a single cup quivered slightly as the tiny witch peeled herself off the curved surface, stood up, and inhaled deeply to inflate herself back to a three-dimensional form. She launched off the edge of the shelf on her broom, flying swiftly to the basement door, which stood slightly ajar. After listening for a moment, she slipped into the space, descending into the shadows below.

He told her what to expect: a dingy, cluttered cave full of junk. But he had also given her a word. *Asperio*.

Her voice was nothing more than the whine of a mosquito.

The utterance opened a tunnel no larger than a pinprick. But it was enough for her to see and to listen undetected.

Long minutes passed before she zoomed away again, this time landing on the musical chessboard. Although some of the pieces were taller than her own form, the tiny green-skinned woman picked each one up, struggling to clear them all away until only the pawns stood in their proper places.

Starting at the column for Middle C, she arranged them one by one. When she was done, the witch picked up her broom and tapped the corner of the chessboard three times. Each pawn levitated individually and came down on the polished wood with a sharp tap.

When the last pawn landed, the witch climbed on her broom again and began to investigate the store, examining the merchandise, flying into the storeroom, and then moving around inside Tori's micro apartment. The tiny crone didn't have to return to her prison on the cup until the humans came back, and she planned to enjoy every second of her freedom.

In a dimly lit study

The man looked up from his book at the sound of the pawns scratching against the surface of the chessboard. Setting the volume aside, he crossed the room and studied the pattern of the pieces. A miniature harp sat beside the board. Tapping the instrument with an elegant forefinger, the man whispered, "*Interpretetur.*"

The strings of the harp vibrated and a clear voice sang, "Come on in, baby take your coat off."

Frowning, the man opened a laptop on the desk, went to a search engine and entered the words. While the message was clear enough, the origin of the lyrics eluded him until four rather hairy men with startlingly white teeth appeared on the screen. Some country and western group from the Eighties called The Oak Ridge Boys.

It shouldn't have come as a surprise. She had, after all, tried to double cross him to acquire a lock of Elvis Presley's hair believed to convey upon the holder the gift of mesmerizing vocal ability -- with a 100 lb. weight gain and some addictive tendencies, side effects best left unmentioned.

That nonsense aside, however? The store was empty, which, as the great Sherlock Holmes himself would have said, meant the game was now afoot.

11

Just as we were about ready to fall in behind Myrtle, I heard frantic squealing, and turned to see Rodney descending the stairs in bounding leaps. He had a little pack of his own strapped to his back. As he skidded to a stop in front of me, I grinned down at him and said, "You want to go, too, little man?"

Rodney nodded vigorously, swiveling his head anxiously between Myrtle and me.

"It's okay with me," I said. "Myrtle?"

"Of course," she said, "We leave no rat behind."

That's Myrtle for you. Just when you think she really is going all Stern Library Lady on us, she cracks a joke. Still, I couldn't shake the feeling that Myrtle was on edge about something, which could not be a good thing.

But, between her joke and Rodney doing a victory dance worthy of an NFL quarterback, any tension in the room evaporated.

I put my hand down. Rodney jumped into my palm, went right up my arm, and stationed himself on the back of my pack. I twisted my neck to look at him over my shoulder. "You good back there?"

Rodney held up one tiny toe as if saying, "Hang on." He extracted a minuscule safety cord from one of the pockets on his backpack, clipped himself to the shoulder strap of my bag, and gave me a thumbs up.

Your guess is as good as mine. Rat Scouts maybe?

"Okay," I said to Myrtle, "lead off."

The group fell in behind her as she began to thread her way through the maze of shelves. Amity walked directly behind Myrtle, Tori came next with Darby, and that left me, Chase, Fetus and Rodney to bring up the rear.

Chase and I could hardly have a personal conversation with that many sharp, furry ears listening, so we made small talk.

"How long have you been going to The Valley?" I asked.

Chase shifted his pack more comfortably on his shoulders, which elicited some grumbling from Festus who was pretending to be napping.

"Remember I told you that I was raised in Raleigh?" Chase said.

"Yes," I said, "I remember. You said Festus left Briar Hollow when he was just a kid."

"Kitten," the old cat corrected me.

"Dad," Chase commanded, "take a nap." Then to me he added, "Sorry. He's just giving you a hard time."

"Grumpy old tomcats don't impress me," I said, purposely setting out to ruffle Festus' fur. It worked.

"I am *not* grumpy," he growled, "and I am not *old*. I've only used up one of my nine lives."

Nine. Lives.

I looked at Chase. "You really live nine lives?"

"That's just the way people put it," he answered, "but all Fae live longer than humans."

That was when I said to myself, "*Okay, girl, you're either in or you're not.*" What I said to Chase, in a perfectly neutral tone, was, "So, how old are you?"

He seemed uncertain how to answer, and then I saw his version of the "in or out" thought move through his eyes. He looked a little bit like he was steeling himself for a blow, but he answered me. "I'll be 87 next month."

"And hairball back there?" I asked calmly.

"Hey!" Festus said. "Watch your language, young lady!"

Chase barely smothered a laugh. "Dad is just shy of 110."

"Really?" I said. "I would have pegged him for 125 if he's a day."

This time Chase did laugh. Festus stood up, turned around three times, and settled back down with his back firmly toward me.

"I think your father is sulking," I told Chase with a grin.

"He does that a lot," Chase agreed. He clearly hadn't expected this conversation to go well. His face betrayed an absolutely adorable mixture of relief, surprise, and hope.

"So, exactly how long do werecats live?" I asked.

"It depends on how much time we spend in the in between," he said, "but the average is around 200."

That was when the "what am I" question moved to the forefront of my thoughts.

I knew Myrtle was ancient, and obviously Darby had been hanging around a long time, but I hadn't give any greater thought than that to Fae lifespans, much less my own. Aunt Fiona was 72 when she died, which made her 17 years older than my mother . . .

"I can almost hear you doing the mental math," Chase said, interrupting my thoughts. "You're wondering if witches live longer, too. The answer is that it varies by practitioner. The more powerful the witch, the longer they live."

That made sense. Life itself is a form of power; it just gets doled out in different measure. I remember learning in high school science class that there's a kind of mayfly that only lives 5 minutes. I guess even when you're an insect, it's what you *do* with those 5 minutes that really counts.

"But am I human or am I Fae?" I asked, sounding as reluctant to know as I felt.

"Uh, Myrtle," Chase said, "you want to take that one?"

The group stopped, and Myrtle turned to face me. "You are a being of the Universe," she said, "one among many beings. There is infinite beauty in variety, Jinx. Those you know as 'humans' are but one branch of the expression of life. I am another; Chase and Festus are another again. As is Darby, and little Rodney. You will live according to the measure of what has been allotted to you, and then your energy will transform and you will live again. That is the way of Creation. 'Fae' and 'human' are nothing but constructs of language. Mere words do not speak to the quality of heart and mind. Do you understand?"

Oddly enough, I did. Some truths simply slip into place in your understanding. That's what Myrtle's explanation did for me. As we continued walking, it wasn't so much the state of my own being that preoccupied my thoughts as trying to understand why the Creavit bartered for immortality.

"The real problem with the Creavit is that what they want to be goes against the natural order of things, isn't it?" I finally asked.

"Yes," Myrtle said. "They want more than what is their allotted measure, and what they seek to do with it disrupts the natural order."

"And it's not just the fact that they want to live longer," Chase said. "Over the span of many lifetimes the Creavit can gain untold wealth and influence. That kind of longevity has its positives and negatives, but it's fantastic for political manipulation and long-range financial planning."

Pieces of the puzzle slowly started to fall into place for me.

"Which would explain how Brenna Sinclair managed to buy a building on the square even if her powers are gone," I said.

"I would imagine so," Chase agreed. "She would have money and resources socked away in accounts with right of survivorship. Immortals get very good at playing human games to pass as normal. They may be powerful Fae, but they have to be careful not to give themselves away. That's how witch hunts get started."

"If they're immortal, why would they care?" I asked.

"Disruption of that sort is literally bad for business," he answered. "The Creavit are power brokers. They prefer to work largely behind the scenes. Societal chaos, burning pyres, and angry Hereditarium councils are not good for their bottom line. Back during the Fae Reformation there were enough Creavit to band together and threaten prevailing power structures. In modern times, most of them are sole practitioners. In fact, that's why my grandfather moved us to Raleigh, to surveil a Creavit."

He dropped that little bombshell like it was the most casual thing in the world, but I was so taken aback, I almost tripped over my own feet.

"What?!" I said. "There are more Creavit in North Carolina?"

Realizing he was yet again hitting me with a potential overload of information, Chase hastened to downplay what he'd just said.

"More like North America now," he assured me, "and there's just the one that we know about. A man named Irenaeus Chesterfield. He's the reason Dad is lame."

From the depth of Chase's pack, Festus declared crossly, "I could have taken him in a fair fight."

If Festus had been anything like Chase in his mountain lion

form, he must have been formidable. And gutsy to take on a Creavit wizard.

"What happened?" I asked.

"Chesterfield tried to gain control of the General Assembly in Raleigh," Chase explained. "He's a classic example of a Creavit who likes to play politics. He wanted all the land up here in the mountains. He figured if he owned it all and developed it, sooner or later he'd find the aos sí and get into The Valley."

From the head of the line, Myrtle said curtly, "Irenaeus Chesterfield is a power hungry fool, or he was, until Festus taught him a lesson."

Curiosity might have killed the cat, but it wasn't doing me a lot of good either. "Would one of you just tell the story, please?" I asked.

"Dad?" Chase asked.

"Go ahead," Festus said tersely. "I was there. I know how it comes out."

"It was June 1936," Chase said. "Congress was just about to green light the Blue Ridge Parkway project under the authority of the National Park Service. Irenaeus was on a train headed to Washington with a bag full of bribe money. Dad and Moira stopped the train right at the Virginia border. It was just supposed to be a delaying tactic. They caused a landslide and covered the tracks with boulders, but Irenaeus detected Moira's presence. He was so intent on reaching his destination that he was willing to risk exposing his powers. He and Moira dueled in a clearing a few hundred yards into the forest."

No longer able to contain himself, Festus sat up in his compartment. He snagged the zipper pull with one extended claw, drew open the flap, and stuck his head out.

"Damned Creavit fool," he said indignantly. "All those humans right there milling around the tracks and he challenges an Alchemist to a duel. Irenaeus had Moira's back to a cliff when

I charged him. Took a bolt of lightning to the hip. Melted the bone in the socket, but I bought Moira the time she needed to bind Irenaeus and hold him. The whole thing was a mess to clean up. She had to put alternate memories in the minds of all the humans who were there. After all that, I will just be damned if I can understand why Barnaby let Irenaeus go."

Myrtle answered him. "Festus, you know perfectly well why Barnaby freed Irenaeus," she said. "The immediate alternative would have been to imprison him in The Valley. The problem with housing a poisonous viper you cannot kill is that sooner or later, he will strike at you. Barnaby thought it was better to allow Irenaeus to play his minor games in human society, but to live under the constant threat of true retribution."

"Wait a minute," I said. "The Creavit are immortal. What could Barnaby possibly do to this Irenaeus guy that would be any kind of major threat?"

Myrtle stopped and turned toward me. The look on her face made the hair on the back of my neck stand up.

"There are many layers to the in between," she said quietly. "Not all are as pleasant as the one you are about to see."

Oh.

"Irenaeus understands that he was afforded considerable mercy," she continued. "It has been years since he's done more than collect rare books and buy and sell antiques. Irenaeus Chesterfield is no longer a threat to The Valley."

EARLIER THAT SUMMER

BRENNA SMILED at the screen hovering in front of her. "The years have been kind to you, Irenaeus," she said. "You look well."

The face of the man who looked back at her was handsome,

in the refined and arrogant manner of an aristocrat. His lips curled in a slow smile.

"Brenna Sinclair," he said. "My, my, my. Done playing magical games with the native savages, have you?"

"Quite to the contrary," she purred. "The games have just begun."

12

Right on the heels of Myrtle's assurances about Irenaeus Chesterfield, she announced, "We're here." I had been so engrossed in the story about Festus and the Creavit wizard, I hadn't been paying attention to our progress through the basement. Glancing at my watch, I realized we'd spent the greater part of an hour reaching the spot where we now stood, right in front of a very ordinary looking door.

Apparently Tori was thinking about how far we'd walked, too. She looked down at Darby and asked, "You've been organizing everything down here in this huge space all by yourself?"

"Yes, Mistress Tori," he said looking up at her, anxious as ever to please, "but if you want me to use a different system I will start over."

Tori turned and stared back down the long aisle between the shelves. We could no longer see the faint glow from the lamps in the area we called the 'lair,' even though we'd followed a straight line.

"No, Darby," she assured him, "I'm sure your system is fine. How is everything arranged?"

"The way Dewey would do it," he answered promptly.

Tori and I were both library nerds in high school. The board finally scraped up enough funds to computerize the school library our junior year. We made extra money over the summer helping Mrs. Hayhurst set up the digital card catalog. She was already north of 70 at the time and refused to give up the old trays of index cards, which were just transferred to a side room. Whenever a kid would ask for a book, Mrs. H. ducked in there and looked it up the old-fashioned way.

"Darby," I asked, "Where did you learn the Dewey decimal system?"

He looked at me like I was speaking Greek. "What is a decimal, Mistress?"

Okay. So this was going to be one of *those* conversations.

"Never mind," I said, deciding to try a different route. "Who is Dewey?"

Darby's face brightened. "Dewey is my best friend," he said. "He is Moira's assistant. Dewey is a dwarf."

Probably one of seven.

Myrtle took that as her cue to both jump in and get us moving again. "*Dewey*," she said, "is someone you will meet shortly if we can quit wasting time and step into the valley."

Even though reaching Shevington was the reason for this whole excursion, my stomach still did a sudden, unexpected flip-flop.

"How does this work?" I asked. "It's not going to be like a roller coaster ride or anything, is it? Because I'm not big on roller coasters."

Chase slipped his hand into mine. "All we have to do is step through the door and we're there," he assured me. "Sometimes it feels a little bit like you're trying to walk into a strong wind, but it won't hurt you. Just put your head down and push through."

Myrtle took a large, brass key out of the pocket of her sweater and inserted it into the lock. When she turned the key, the tumblers in the mechanism moved smoothly, allowing her to draw the door back on its hinges revealing ... a blank wall.

That is, until she raised her hand, chanted something soft and sing-songy under her breath, and a rippling oval of light formed in the center of the doorway. As it flowed outward, sunlight streamed into the basement. On the other side of the opening, I saw a beautiful mountain meadow.

"Holy freaking Narnia, Batman," Tori whispered.

Myrtle looked at me, gesturing with a sweep of her hand indicating that I should enter first. At that instant, thanks to Tori's reaction to the portal, something Aslan said popped into my head, "To defeat the darkness out there, you must defeat the darkness in yourself."

Nerves or not, I knew I was moving toward a place filled with light.

Chase described the physical sensation well. For just a second I strained against an invisible barrier, and then I was through and standing in a world scrubbed clean of everything that coats our reality -- the grime of "progress."

The scent of blooming flowers flavored the air. Closing my eyes, I turned my face toward the sun. Around me, birds sang merrily in the trees and off somewhere in the distance, I heard the bleat of grazing sheep. The burbled notes of running water rose up in the natural song, playing over a bass line of indolent, buzzing bees. The moment flowed like the opening movement of a symphony. There was no sense of time or distance, only the mesmerizing *difference* that is The Valley.

From behind me I heard a barely muffled cough. I stood frozen in place, blocking the entrance for the others.

When I moved aside, Tori came through and had exactly the same reaction. I had to take her by the elbow and drag her out of the way.

Chase and Festus were next, then Amity and Darby, and

finally Myrtle. But this was not the slightly severe, basically monochrome, bespectacled librarian with whom we spent so much time. This was Myrtle in her true form, ever young, lithe, regal, emanating a golden glow of her own.

"Myrtle," Tori said, "has anyone ever told you that you're a real looker?"

The musical lilt of Myrtle's laugh danced around us. "Several someones over many lifetimes," she said. "Welcome to the Valley of Shevington."

I felt Chase's eyes on me and looked over at him. "Kinda blows you away the first time, huh?" he asked, grinning.

"The first time?" I asked in a stunned voice. "Do you ever get used to it?"

To my surprise it was Festus who answered.

"You do not," he assured me, his usual raspy voice striking a gentler tone.

In a purely practical sense, the meadow below the town of Shevington has all the technical features of any meadow. But that's where the comparison stops. The colors are more vibrant than anything in our part of the world. The grass beneath your feet pulsates with the greenness of life. And the sky overhead? Well, it's . . . *limpid*.

I honestly can say I'd ever even *thought* that word until that exact moment, but trust me, when you see *limpid* blue for the first time, your brain supplies the right descriptive.

It's more than the colors, the clean air, the blooming flowers, the slight whiff of fires from the city itself. There is something uniquely, transcendently Shevington. I've been to the Valley many times now and I still can't give that redolence a name.

As my senses began to adjust, I took note of my immediate surroundings. Shevington proper lay about half a mile ahead, nestled in a rugged mountain cleft. Gray stone walls surrounded the city, glinting brightly in the sunlight. Initially, we thought we were looking at flecks of gold until Myrtle explained that the granite in the mountains contains pyrite deposits.

You may have figured out by now that just because I had come into my powers, I wasn't exactly running around using them every day. Any new discoveries in that regard had to pretty much land at my feet, which is precisely what happened next.

A sound overhead attracted my attention. I looked up to see a small flock of six miniature dragons circling over us. I heard a worried "eep" from Rodney as he hastily shrugged out of his tiny pack and ducked under my shirt collar.

"It's okay, buddy," I said, giving his head a soothing pat, "nobody is going to hurt you."

Myrtle looked up and said, "Ah, *Draco Americanus Minor*, the New World variant of *Draco Europa Major*."

She might as well have had binoculars around her neck and a copy of *The Field Guide to Dragons of North America* in her hand.

As we watched the creatures dip and circle, Tori said, "So that's 'draco' as in 'dragon,' right?"

"Dragonlets," Myrtle corrected her, in the same clinical tone. "They're quite harmless and rather attracted to the company of the Fae. Many creatures considered to be mythological by humankind have found sanctuary here in The Valley."

As if to prove her point, and completely without warning, the dragonlets all dove at the same time, landing in front of me in a straight line, their curved talons digging into the dirt as they grounded themselves. They were roughly the size of large dogs, covered with blue and purple iridescent scales. Tilting their bird-like heads to the side and regarding me through faceted, amber eyes, the dragonlets spread their wings and bowed low, touching the earth with their beaks. Adrenaline-charged fear rushed through my veins until I realized that the rumbling sound I heard from them was purring.

Curious, I started to step forward, only to be stopped by

furious chattering from the depths of my collar. Rodney didn't want me getting anywhere near the dragonlets. One of the creatures looked up with a hungry gleam in his eye. "Okay," I said, "we are getting something straight right now. Rodney is off limits. He is *not* a menu item and you will not hurt him, got it?"

All six dragonlets raised their heads and nodded. "Okay, Rodney," I said, "suck it up, we're going in." I approached the first dragonlet, held out my hand, and began petting its head. The purring increased to a thrumming roar. Moving down the line, I petted each one in turn, until they were all staring at me with open adoration. I turned around to say something to Myrtle only to discover that she, Chase, Amity, and Tori were staring at me -- with their jaws hanging open.

"What?" I asked.

Myrtle recovered first. "When I said that dragonlets enjoyed the company of the Fae," she said, "I meant that they are content to live in proximity to the city. I have never seen any member of any magical race tame a dragonlet."

What can I say? I carted a snapping turtle home from the river when I was a kid and insisted on keeping it over my mother's dire predictions of lost fingers and bloody stumps. I fed Boxy by hand and she never even tried to bite me. For the record, do not try that at home.

"Uh, I've always been good with animals?" I offered lamely.

"That," Myrtle said, "would appear to be something of an understatement. I know your powers have depths you have not yet plumbed, but you are proving to be a constant wonder, Jinx."

I have to tell you, I wasn't sure I was thrilled about that, and I was less thrilled discussing it in front of everyone. Thankfully, Darby came to the rescue. Out of the corner of my eye, I saw him fidgeting next to Tori. Scratch that. Squirming. Perfect. Just the change of topic I needed.

"You really want us to get a move on, don't you, Darby?" I asked.

He looked like a kid who just got caught with his hand in the candy jar. "Oh, no, Mistress," he hastily assured me. "I just . . . had . . . an . . . itch."

I grinned at him. "Itching to see your friend is more like it," I said. "I'm sorry. We haven't been thinking about how much this trip means to you."

Turning back to Myrtle, I asked, "Do I need to . . . dismiss . . . the dragonlets or something?"

Myrtle eyed the creatures that were still sitting quietly on the ground watching my every move. "I think we should leave that up to them," she suggested. With a gesture toward the path, she added, "Shall we?"

13

I hadn't taken two steps before the dragonlets rose into the air and settled into a perfect "V" formation over our heads.

Tori moved up beside me. "You're stepping up from bringing stray cats home," she observed wryly.

"Let's just hope there's no litter box training involved with this crew," I replied.

Ahead of us, Myrtle and Amity were talking quietly, but I couldn't make out what they were saying. I did hear Festus behind me declare loudly, and in a highly annoyed voice, "Boy, it is none of your business how much time I do or don't spend in a pub."

Chase tried to pitch his voice low, but his words still came through. "Dad, I would just like to avoid a repeat of the *incident* that happened during our last visit to The Valley. It's pretty embarrassing to have to spring you from the local gaol."

I didn't need a dictionary to figure out that "gaol" was a 75-cent word for "jail." It took all of my self-restraint not to giggle.

And then he said something so sweet, I had to resist the urge to turn around and hug him.

"Would you please just behave yourself this one time for

me?" Chase asked. "I'm trying to make a good impression on Jinx. That's kind of hard to do with you catting around in some werecat dive."

"The Dirty Claw is not a dive," Festus said defensively. "It's a retired gentleman's drinking establishment."

"Right," Chase hissed, "where retired gentlemen werecats smoke catnip, drink creamed whisky, and caterwaul at the top of their lungs."

"You know, boy," Festus said amiably and loudly, "you really ought to do something about that hairball stuck up your . . ."

Before Festus could finish the thought, I hastily called out, "Hey, Myrtle, can I ask a question?"

As Myrtle told me to go ahead, I heard Chase whisper furiously behind me, "We will finish this conversation *later*, Dad."

Parents. They *will* grow up to embarrass their kids.

I had been studying the landscape while I eavesdropped, and I really did have a question. "Why don't these mountains look like the ones around Briar Hollow?" I asked.

"They are the same mountains," Myrtle replied, "but remember, they developed along a different path of time."

That didn't mean a lot to me and I would have been willing to let the answer go at face value, but Tori was determined to understand the whole alternate chronology question.

"I thought the two time streams were parallel," she said.

"The streams are parallel, but they are not identical," Myrtle replied. "They flow side by side, but events affect the depth and nature of each stream. This is a line of time in which the land you think of as North Carolina remained remote and wild. It was subject to a variant of the forces that formed the mountains, one that was more violent and forceful. Barnaby chose this stream for those very reasons."

We took a few more steps, during which I could almost hear the gears turning in Tori's mind. "Are you saying that the Valley of Shevington is the only settlement in this time stream?" she asked.

When Myrtle answered, there was a note of approval in her voice. "Very good," she said. "You are correct. It might be most accurate to think of Shevington as an island in the river of time."

I have no doubt Tori could have taken that conversation all the way to the gates of the city, but a booming voice stopped us dead in our tracks. "HALT! Who goes there?"

We were just a few yards from an arched, rock bridge over the stream that bisects The Valley. A short, disheveled looking old man with a straggly chin beard blocked our way.

Myrtle regarded him with threadbare tolerance. "Bill Ruff," she said, "you know exactly who I am. Now step aside."

"Not until you've paid the toll," the man barked.

"That will be enough guff out of you," Myrtle shot back. "If you don't get out of my way this instant, I'll turn you right back into a goat."

Tori and I looked at each other.

"Bill Ruff?" she mouthed.

"Billy Goat Gruff?" I mouthed back.

It never occurred to me the old coot could hear us, but Bill Ruff had sharp ears and a sharper tongue. "Don't be associating me with that ridiculous fairy tale," he growled.

"Bill is a bit thin skinned," Myrtle observed mildly. "He never has been able to take a joke." She raised her right hand, one slender index finger held aloft. "Shall we write a sequel to that bit of fiction, Bill?"

The old man obviously didn't like it, but he stepped aside. As we passed him, I heard some muttering that sounded like "smug, superior aos sí," but I couldn't be positive and I *certainly* wasn't going to ask Myrtle. I didn't want that index finger pointed at me.

The ground from the bridge sloped up to the wooden gate of

the city. Celtic symbols adorned the black iron bands holding the massive planks in place.

As we stood there regarding the gate, the dragonlets hovered expectantly over our heads. Shading my eyes with my hand, I looked up at them. "You all go on home now," I said. "I'll call you if I need you for anything."

I had no idea why I might *need* a dragonlet, but I was relieved when the creatures did as they were told and flew away.

As her eyes roamed over the gate, Tori said, "So, is this the part where we get to answer three questions before we can enter?"

"Don't be silly," Myrtle scoffed in clipped tones, "you've seen *Monty Python* too many times."

Which was true.

At any rate, the gate opened of its own accord and a scene straight out of a Renaissance Faire greeted us. Men and women in modern dress moved up and down the main thoroughfare talking with their friends and neighbors who were attired in more or less Medieval clothing. Over the course of our stay, I came to understand that many of the inhabitants of Shevington spend time in our world. The people of The Valley are in no way removed from the 21st century world of humans. Quite the opposite, in fact. Trust me, you'll see what I mean. Right now, let's get back to the story.

Just like the countryside, the town is impeccably clean. The shops offer an eclectic assortment of wares. My eye went immediately to the leather-bound volumes sitting nestled in purple velvet arranged in the bookseller's window. In keeping with the theme, amethyst geodes weighted the covers of some of the books, holding them open to display luxuriant, hand-dyed endpapers.

Old-fashioned fountain pens lay among the books, ornately overlaid with gold scrollwork and studded with precious stones.

Bottles of ink sat in a carefully arranged pyramid off to one side. The placard in the window, written in flowing script read, "Books bound to bear witness to incantations, secrets, and recipes. - *H.H. Pagecliff, Propr.*"

Just across the street, an open air-cafe reminiscent of the streets of Paris, played host to assorted patrons. Some were engaged in lively conversation, while others were bent over game boards or absorbed in their reading. The scene could have been straight out of our own espresso bar, except we don't typically serve the drinks by levitating them over the crowd and gently landing the cups in front of the customers.

There were food carts selling fresh fruit, vegetables, and hot dishes that smelled so enticing my mouth watered. As we watched, a young man whizzed by on a skateboard -- that was hovering about six inches off the ground.

I heard the sound of hooves on the cobblestones, and then Tori gasped, clutched my arm and pointed with her free hand. "Is that what I think it is?" she whispered.

Since the moment we'd found out about my powers, Tori kept asking one question. "Are unicorns real?"

She was looking at her answer.

The man leading the unicorn mare must have seen the expression on Tori's face, because he brought the creature over to us, smiling kindly at Tori who was trembling with excitement.

"Have you never seen one of the beasties before, miss?" he asked. He tipped his cap to Myrtle and said, "Good day to you, aos sí."

Myrtle answered him with a gentle smile. "And to you, kind sir," she said. "May my young friend pet the mare?"

"Of course," he said. "She's gentle as a lamb, this one."

No matter what else I might have grappled with over coming to terms with the existence of the magical world and my growing role in it, that moment watching Tori made it all worth it. She reached out with both hands, gently laying them on either side of the unicorn's muzzle.

"Hello, pretty girl," Tori whispered. "Do you know you just made my dream come true?"

The unicorn bobbed its head up and down.

"You do know, don't you," Tori crooned. "Are we going to be friends?"

The animal nickered, lowered her head, and delicately rested it against Tori's shoulder, being exquisitely careful with the twisted horn in the center of her forehead. Tori wrapped her arms around the unicorn's neck. "What's your name, darling?"

"Her name is Blissia," the man said, "and I'm Ellis Groomsby, head stableman of Shevington. You come to the stables any time, miss. They're just down at the end of the main row here. Go to the left at the bottom of the hill toward the grove of trees and you'll find us."

He tipped his cap and Tori reluctantly released her hold on the unicorn. "I'll see you later, Blissia," she whispered, "and I'll bring you an apple." Then, catching herself, she looked up at Ellis. "Can I bring her an apple?"

"Best be bringing two, miss," the man laughed. "This one's got quite the sweet tooth."

Tori watched as Ellis led the unicorn away, pure joy filling her features. "They *are* real," she said. "Unicorns are real."

I've seen Tori's bucket list and a lot of the things on there are kind of impossible -- or at least I thought they were until I watched my BFF hug a unicorn.

Amity put her arm around Tori's shoulder. "I'll walk down to the stables with you after supper," she said. "I like the unicorns, too, but the griffons are my favorite."

"Humph," Festus snorted. "Griffons. Can't make up their minds if they want to be cats or birds. Damned nuisance. Why in the name of Bastet would anyone want a creature that sheds *and* molts?"

"Ignore him," Amity said. "I think he's overdue for his worming."

That won her a furious glare. "Put me down, boy," Festus commanded. "I have my own business to attend to."

"Dad," Chase hedged, "don't you want to come with us to the center of town and at least say hello to Barnaby and Moira?"

"I'll be along before the talking starts," Festus said. "Now put me down."

Heaving a resigned sigh, Chase went down on one knee. Festus hopped out of the pack, making a perfect three-point landing. He shook out his fur and limped off down a side street without another word.

"Let me guess," I said sympathetically, "The Dirty Claw is down that way."

Chase's face fell. "You heard?" he said.

"We all have parents, Chase," I answered, trying to hide my grin. "You have to let them grow up sometime."

That won a round of laughter from the whole group, which seemed to put Chase at ease. "Don't ever tell Dad I said so, but they can be an entertaining bunch of old coots," he said ruefully. " Just imagine a pack of half-drunk tomcats stoned on nip trying to out lie each other. And the worst part is that I'm related to most of them."

"You can't pick your relatives," I consolingly.

Little did Chase know it, but he would be taking me to The Dirty Claw.

A tomcat bar, with actual, *feline* tomcats who are *related* to Chase? No *way* I was missing that.

We followed Myrtle though the streets of Shevington. As we drew closer to the center of the city, I became aware of Dílestos. The staff had been so instantly familiar in my hand; I'd been carrying it all that time without much thought. Now, however, the wood seemed to quiver in my grasp.

When I asked Myrtle about it, she said, "The staff senses the nearness of the Mother Tree -- her mother. She anticipates the reunion with joy."

Until we rounded a corner and stepped into the central square, I didn't know that I was about to experience a reunion of my own. Aunt Fiona stood at the base of the Mother Tree, in full, *living* color.

14

If we'd been in a movie, I'd have done something like run forward in slow motion while poignant music swelled in the background as I threw my arms around my aunt. Yeah, well, we were shy a choreographer to work out the whole dramatic reunion. Instead, I sort of stumbled in her direction and blurted out like a complete idiot, "You're *alive*?"

Aunt Fiona smiled at me brightly. "Oh, yes, dear. I'm afraid we've been playing . . . well, sort of a game of charades."

Except she conveniently forgot to tell me it was a game.

"But, you showed up in my kitchen, all pale and . . . and . . . *glowy*," I protested. "We *buried* you. Wait. Who did we bury?"

Looking mildly offended, Aunt Fiona said, "You buried a facsimile of me, which is the only reason I didn't protest that pink polyester funeral garb your mother picked out." She paused and let out with a wounded sniffle. "If I didn't know better, it almost sounds like you wish I *were* dead."

I groaned inwardly. Aunt Fiona was not without the same drama queen streak that drove me nuts in my mom.

"Don't be ridiculous," I said. "I don't wish you were dead. I'm very glad to see you."

That's when I hugged her.

I *was* glad to see her, but I also wanted to verify that she was, indeed, in the world of the living. With an Aunt Fiona story, fact checking is generally a good thing.

When I stepped back, I smiled at her, and said, "I just don't understand how you managed the whole . . . charade. You were pretty convincing."

Mollified by the compliment, Fiona answered happily, "I was, wasn't I? Have you ever heard the expression 'smoke and mirrors?' Well, that's how we did it."

That was an opening to actually get some details.

"We?" I prodded.

"Moira helped me," Fiona said. "We used one of her magical mirrors to project my image across the in between into our regular time stream. Well, the stream where the store is. You know what I mean. Think of it like one of those holo-tele-micro-gram . . . things."

In spite of myself, I smiled. "Hologram," I said. "But holo-grams can't interact with their environment, Aunt Fiona. You moved things. You petted my cats. How did you pull that off?"

Fiona blinked at me as if I'd just asked something incredibly silly. "Well, dear," she said a little patronizingly, "it *is* a very *good* projector. After all, it belongs to an Alchemist."

Right. I knew that.

Exchanges like this with Aunt Fiona can circle around and go nowhere for hours. I opted to leave well enough alone and sort out the details later. Instead, I went after the motive.

"Would I be completely out of line if I asked you to at least tell me *why* you decided to impersonate a ghost?" I asked.

"Oh, that's simple, dear," Fiona said. "There were two reasons. First, I wanted to move to Shevington full time, and I wanted you to have the store, which was so much easier to do if I played dead. The legal system can be so annoying."

She paused, pursing the corners of her mouth as if she were about to confess something huge. "And, well, I have to admit I hoped that living with Myrtle might inspire you to discover and embrace your true heritage. I never dreamed you'd ask for your magic so quickly and put all of this in motion. You've saved us *ever* so much time dear."

Yeah. Go me. One half-awake "sort of" request and look what it got me.

By this time, Myrtle and the others had joined us. Chase swept Fiona up in a big hug, lifting her off the ground and twirling her around in a circle while she giggled like a girl. When he put her back down, he said, with mock sternness, "*You* are a rascal."

Amity shook her finger at Fiona. "You could have told *me* at least," she scolded.

"Oh," Fiona said, her eyes going wide, "I couldn't do *that* Amity. You never have been able to keep your mouth shut."

Tori was next up for a hug, and then Myrtle and Fiona clasped hands. My aunt said something in Gaelic I didn't understand. Myrtle answered in the same language, and then they both turned and smiled at me.

I regarded them both with raised eyebrows. "Okay, you two," I said, "I'm guessing there's a whole lot more to this story."

Myrtle laughed. "Yes, there is a great deal more. I would like to apologize for my role in Fiona's 'charade.' All I can tell you is that it was for the best. Now that you know why your mother chose to turn her back on her ancestry, surely you can understand that her decision complicated things for us in working with you."

That was fair.

"You have surprised us at every turn," Myrtle went on. "None of the events of this summer have been orchestrated. You've handled everything that has been thrown at you in a manner that has far exceeded our expectations. We've tried to both help you with the immediate circumstances with which you have been presented and prepare you for all of this at the same time."

She circumscribed a circle with a wave of her hand.

All of this.

Shevington.

A different stream of time. A different world. Metaphysical politics. Good witches. Bad witches.

Suddenly a gentle whisper stirred in my mind. "They did the best they could."

Startled, I looked around. "Who said that?" I asked.

"I did," the voice spoke again.

In my hand, Dílestos quivered.

What had I been thinking? We were standing under the spreading branches of the Mother Tree. I let myself get so preoccupied with Aunt Fiona's smoke and mirrors I forgot where I was.

Let's pause for some factoids. General Sherman, a giant sequoia in California, is the biggest tree by volume in the world. It's about 2,000 years old and stands just less than 275 feet. That's enough mass to take up about half of an Olympic-sized swimming pool. The *tallest* tree in the world is a California redwood that tops out around 380 feet. At only 800 years, it's a gangly teenager compared to the General, but it's higher than the Statue of Liberty.

The Mother Tree makes them both look like saplings.

Standing in her presence, you know her roots reach to the bedrock. The gentleness of the tree's voice belies the solidity and grace of her connection to the beating heart of the earth. Her wisdom resonates with the timbre of gravity more than gravitas. The Mother Tree compels communion. For all the breadth of her knowledge, she courses with curiosity. While her patience is immense, no measure can gauge her compassion and interest. She exists to learn.

It may seem silly, but I opened my mind to her and said the first thing that occurred to me. "I'm sorry I was ignoring you."

"With good reason," the answer came. "A ghost come back to life demands notice."

I started to ask a question, and then stopped myself. The Mother Tree heard me anyway.

"You are here as I am here," she said. "To learn. Attend to those who approach. Come to me when you wish to speak."

The Mother Tree didn't point, but I still knew in which direction to look. A man and a woman strode toward us over the expanse of verdant lawn accompanied by . . . R2D2?

I blinked and squinted. At a distance, whatever the third figure was looked exactly like a rolling barrel. Then the breeze caught a long, white beard and blew it out to one side. The 'barrel' was a stout little man trundling forward on stumpy legs. He was almost as thick as he was tall. As they drew nearer, I made out a grin splitting his aged, merry face. Then he raised one stubby hand and waved excitedly to Darby.

The little brownie couldn't contain himself. He broke into a run, tackling his friend enthusiastically. They went down on the grass, rolling in a happy ball.

"I'm guessing that's Dewey," Tori said in a bemused voice.

"Gee, ya think?" I laughed.

The couple coming toward us stepped around Dewey and Darby. As they neared our group, the tall, dark-haired man held out his hand. "I'd say they're happy to see one another, wouldn't you?" He had bright, blue eyes and wore a grizzled, close-cropped beard. "I'm Barnaby Shevington," he said, "and I am delighted to welcome you to our town, Jinx, and you, Tori."

He shook each of our hands in turn, greeted Amity, and then bowed formally to Myrtle, "Well met, aos sí," he said.

"Well met, Lord Mayor," she answered. "Fare thee well?"

"Well, indeed," he replied before holding out his hand to Chase. "Young Master McGregor."

"Hi, Barnaby," Chase grinned. "Ready to lose to me in chess again?"

Barnaby clucked his tongue. "Do not be so confident, young one," he cautioned. "Cigars, brandy, and a game tonight?"

Chase hesitated for just a fraction of a second. Then, gathering his resolve, he said, "I'd like that . . . after I walk the wall with Jinx."

I had no idea what "walking the wall" meant, but I liked it that Chase was putting a kind-of-date with me ahead of the Lord High Mayor. Being made a priority is definitely one way to a girl's heart.

Barnaby took the answer with perfect grace. "Absolutely," he said. "You know I'm a night owl. Come around when you're ready."

Turning back toward Tori, and me Barnaby said, "Please, excuse my bad manners. Allow me to introduce you to our Alchemist, Moira."

Moira is of mixed elven and Druidic descent, which makes her remarkably "handsome." You know, the way the word is applied to women like Angelica Houston? Attractive, but strong and robust. Like Myrtle, Moira is tall, but with none of the lithe, winsomeness that is part of Myrtle's true form. Moira is a woman who looks like she could stand against a raging storm and dare the tempest to move her.

She greeted me as warmly as Barnaby had, but when she took Tori's hand, Moira looked long into her eyes. "Are you ready for this?" Moira asked her.

"I honestly don't know," Tori said, "but I'm game if you are."

A slow smile spread over Moira's face. "My dear child," she said, "I was born game."

"Me, too," Tori replied.

"Would you like to see my workshop this evening after dinner?" Moira asked. "We can discuss both your calling and your training."

"That sounds great," Tori said, "but I want to go to the stables with Amity first."

Moira's smile broadened. "The unicorns?"

Tori nodded happily.

"Good," Moira said, "I'll go with you. I love them, too."

"Excellent," Barnaby said, clapping his hands together. "It would seem the plans for the evening are falling into place of their own accord. You will be staying at the inn next door to my quarters beside the town hall. Allow me to show you all to your rooms so you can rest a bit before we gather for the evening meal. Agreed?"

When Moira excused herself to return to her workshop, Myrtle said, "If you don't mind, Moira, I'd like to come with you and talk for a bit."

"A pleasure as always, aos sí," the Alchemist said.

Aunt Fiona promised to join us for supper, and Chase went off to locate Festus. That left Amity, Tori, Rodney, and me to follow Barnaby to the inn. Darby was nowhere to be seen.

Barnaby introduced us to the innkeeper, Mrs. McElroy, before excusing himself as well. She was a jolly, red-faced woman who talked non-stop as she lumbered up the stairs, first getting Amity settled in a single room and then putting Tori and me in two adjoining rooms.

"I'd be appreciating it if you'd not be working any incantations involving smoke, fire, noise, or noxious odors after 10 o'clock," she said, as she threw the curtains back and flooded our shared sitting area with light. "And will your rat be requiring anything special?"

From his position on my shoulder, Rodney shook his head.

Then he lifted one paw, kissed it, and blew the smooch toward Mrs. McElroy who burst into delighted twittering. "Get on with you then, Sir Rat," she said. "It's a right flirt you are."

Rodney trotted down my arm, hopped onto the back of a chair, executed a gallant bow, and winked at Mrs. McElroy, sending her into another gale of giggles. Something told me there was a hunk of cheese in Rodney's future.

When Tori and I were finally alone, she looked at me and said, "Seriously. We've been in an accident. I hit my head and am massively concussed, right?"

"Nope," I said, putting my pack down. "We're really here and you really petted a unicorn."

"Would I sound like a total moron if I said 'oh my God' like 50 times?" she asked.

"Yes, you would," I assured her, "not to mention irritating. But I get where you're coming from. Can you believe this place?"

Tori flopped down in one of the chairs and held out her arm so Rodney could join her. "How about you, little man?" she asked, peering into his bright, black eyes. "Are you believing this?"

Rodney nodded and held out his paw for a high five, which Tori gently returned with her index finger.

"I guess we really are *not* in freaking Kansas any more," she said.

Taking the chair opposite her, I said, "We've never been to Kansas either."

"God, Jinksy!" she protested. "That is completely *not* relevant. You've got dragons flying around after you, I made friends with a unicorn, and I'm pretty sure you had a heart-to-heart with the great Mother Tree of all trees. You were talking to her, weren't you? Come on. Dish. What did she say?"

"Just that we're here to learn, and that I should go out there and really talk to her when I'm ready," I said.

"Is she like the other trees?" Tori asked.

I shook my head. "No," I said. "She's ancient. I think she's older than Myrtle."

"Which brings up mystery number two," Tori said. "What do you suppose Myrtle and Moira are talking about?"

"What else?" I said. "Our futures. I just hope they're ready to give us some answers. I mean this is all cool, and clearly Shevington is going to be a major part of our lives now, but am I the only person who is worried that Brenna Sinclair is sitting back there in Briar Hollow undoubtedly up to no good?"

Tori stretched in her chair. "You are not," she said, "and I'm not too thrilled about this Irenaeus dude, either. Myrtle can tease me all she wants to, but I'm telling you, arch villains are never done when you think they're done. Penguin, Joker, Magneto, Poison Ivy, Mystique, Lex Luthor. Scumbags like that are hard to put down."

Pardon me if I wasn't comforted by that recitation of comic book . . . excuse me, *graphic novel* . . . bad guys. Unless Batman, Superman, and Wolverine were waiting in the wings to help out, we were the ones who were going to be out there dealing with Brenna and any buddies of hers who happen to show up. I was feeling a whole lot better about my powers -- until Chase told that story about Festus and Moira dueling with Irenaeus Chesterfield.

I distinctly remembered a reference to a lightning bolt *melting* the bone in Festus' hip. *That* experience was definitely not on *my* bucket list. Before I could say so, however, light snoring floated over from the vicinity of Tori's chair. Both she and Rodney were down for the count. It had been a long walk. Maybe I'd just close my eyes for a second, too.

When a light tap on the door awakened me, I was surprised to find the sun had gone down. I glanced around the room looking for a light to turn on. Then it occurred to me that there probably was no electricity in The Valley, at least not the kind involving wiring. As my eyes adjusted to the dimness, I made out the vague shape of a lamp sitting on the table. Purely to be a smart ass, I looked at the lamp, snapped my fingers, and almost fainted with the globe came alive with a bright, golden light.

"Huh, uh, what?" Tori mumbled, blinking in the sudden brightness.

"Check this out," I said, moving to another lamp. I snapped my fingers again and it sprang to life as well.

"Whoa," she said. "Nice one."

The tap at the door sounded again. When I opened it, Amity was standing there. She looked me up and down and said disapprovingly, "I hope you're not planning on having dinner with the Lord High Mayor of Shevington looking like that?"

Busted.

"Sorry," I said. "We fell asleep. Give us 10 minutes and we'll be down."

15

Earlier that summer

The little witch's lack of control amused Brenna. The spirits from the graveyard now milled around the courthouse square growing more confused and restless, searching in vain for a connection with their former lives. Soon their discontent would generate enough energy to make them visible in the living world. Then the real fun would begin. The only thing humans feared more than death was a return of the dead.

Brenna stood beneath the statue of a soldier. She'd read about his war, a doomed economic conflict between the industrial north and the agrarian south. So typically human to erect a monument to a lost cause. She chose the spot purely for its location, directly across the street from the store that embodied the aos sí.

The power of the ancient Fae spirit prevented Brenna from entering the building, but she knew the fledgling witch and her tiny band of misfits could see her. Brenna opened her mind's eye and searched the darkened windows. The girl's aura pulsated like the trembling heart of a terrified bird. It made Brenna smile, which only sent the pathetic creatures shrinking deeper into the shadows. How deliciously amusing it would be to torment that one into submission.

Brenna turned her attention back to the aimless ghosts. Surely one of them would be of use to her. She raised her hand, softly chanting the words of a spell that activated the large ruby set in gold adorning her index finger. Alas, it was not the elusive Philosopher's Stone, but the blood-red gem still served her well. She'd cut it from the finger of an Alchemist who insisted on attempting to thwart her. With the ruby, Brenna could see into the hidden world of motivations.

Still holding her hand aloft, palm out, Brenna scanned the crowd. A few of the ghosts, misinterpreting the gesture, waved at her. Brenna ignored them, concentrating instead on exploring the sins weighing against their eternal slumber. Most of the petty transgressions she found barely qualified as trivial in her estimation.

A Sunday school teacher tormenting herself for taking a few dollars a week from the collection plate to obtain the cigarettes her husband would not allow her to buy even though he drank his own paycheck.

A smattering of garden-variety adulterers.

Some enterprising tax evaders.

Brenna's hand stopped over a man in a disgustingly cheap garment. The pale residue of his living aura bristled with arrogant self-importance. Brenna intensified her scrutiny and found a viable catalog of misdeeds on which she could draw. Land fraud. Election rigging. Gambling. Cheating.

Ah, it was the cheating that did him in. A contest over . . . fish? The fool died by the hand of a man he wronged over the weight of a game fish and the awarding of a cheap hunk of brass. Oh, yes. This one would do nicely.

Brenna glided across the courthouse lawn, the dark cloak falling from her shoulders billowing behind her. The spirits she passed shrank away. Even as pale shades, they feared the sight of the sorceress.

But the one she approached took no notice until Brenna cleared her throat and said, "Pardon my intrusion, sir. You seem the most levelheaded and responsible of this throng. May I ask what has transpired to bring you all here?"

"That's the $10,000 question, lady," he snapped. "The little twit who runs that insufferable Fiona Ryan's store insists I'm dead, which is impossible since I'm following a five-year action plan."

Feigning sympathy, Brenna said, "How incredibly inconvenient for a man of your stature, but I do fear that you are indeed no longer in the world of the living."

"How would you know that?" he blustered.

"I am a sorceress."

"Yeah, right Glenda," he scoffed. "What are you going to do? Wiggle your nose and turn me into a rabbit or something?"

Under normal circumstances, his insolence would have won him a transformation, first into a rabbit, and then into dinner, but Brenna had need of his services.

"I am willing to give you a demonstration," she demurred. "What, pray tell would convince you?"

A speculative gleam came into the man's eye. Looking around, his gaze stopped on a spout rising from the lawn. "Turn that water faucet into gold," he demanded.

Gold. They always wanted gold. From the alchemists to this strange modern world, humans continued to nurse their fascination with that weak, malleable metal.

"Very well," Brenna replied. She focused her power on the material of the spigot, moving her awareness into the mass of minute particles that constituted its substance and that of all matter. Slowly she rearranged their order, altering the orbits and combinations.

As she worked, the hue at the base of the pipe lightened. The discoloration crept upward toward the open mouth of the spigot, where a single drop of water hung suspended, building tension toward its ultimate descent to the wet earth below. Granted, it was a bit of unnecessary showmanship, but Brenna turned the droplet into a glittering diamond.

The ghost beside her gaped at her handiwork. "Holy shit," he said, adding hastily, "pardon my French."

French? His command of that language was thin indeed if he could not even muster the word *merde*.

"Have I convinced you?" Brenna asked.

"Yeah," he greedily, "can you do that again?"

"As many times as you like," Brenna said, "but is that your only goal? Accumulating wealth?"

The man gaped at her. "What else is there?" he asked stupidly.

For just an instant, Brenna considered selecting another of the spirits. This one's dim thought processes required entirely too much patience, but then again, a mind so weak was, like gold itself, enticingly soft.

"Perhaps you would like to regain your life," she suggested.

"Huh," he said, appearing to actually require time to consider her offer. "I guess I can't do anything with that gold if I'm dead, right?"

Brenna inclined her head demurely to one side. "How very perceptive of you . . . "

When the man failed to understand the pause as a prompt to supply his name, Brenna prodded, "I don't know your name."

"Howard McAlpin," he said, puffing out his chest, "mayor of Briar Hollow."

"And I am Brenna Sinclair," she said.

"Nice to meet you," he said perfunctorily. "Now bring me back to life."

Stupid, rude, *and* demanding. No wonder he'd chosen politics as his profession.

"Oh, no, Mr. Mayor," she said, "my magic is not simply at your beck and call."

With a snap of her fingers, she broke the loose threads holding the metal's transformation in place, relishing the disappointment that flooded Howard's face as the gold vanished and the diamond crashed to earth, shattering into a fine, liquid spray.

"If you want your life," she continued, "and enough precious commodities to facilitate the reacquisition of your own brand of power, you must give me something in return."

Dim though he might be, Howard clearly knew a negotiation when he saw one. "What does a dead guy have that a woman like you wants?" he asked.

"Information," Brenna replied.

"About what?"

"The affairs of this town," she said, "and the opportunities they present to complicate the life of the woman who runs that store."

Howard grinned. "Dirt," he said. "That I can give you, and if it screws over Fiona Ryan's niece in the process, I'm good with that. What do you want to know?"

PRESENT TIME

As Brenna watched, Jinx turned on her heel and walked rapidly back toward her own store. At least, the girl didn't quite turn tail and run, although the fact that she had waved proved the depths of her vacuity -- a fact that still made Brenna seethe.

To be stripped of her powers by the likes of Jinx and with the aid of Brenna's own blood! The irony infuriated her. Still, of the two young women, Victoria -- Tori -- had far more inner fire. If her misguided loyalty toward Jinx could be broken, Tori could easily claim her place as the first member of Brenna's own coven.

But that would all come in good time. First there was the matter of getting past the aos sí and into the basement of the store. According to Iranaeus Chesterfield, the space was a treasure trove of magical information and artifacts, and more importantly, the gateway to the Valley of Shevington and the last Alchemist.

Going to the cemetery to confront Jinx and Tori had been a tactical mistake on Brenna's part -- one she would not make again. Nor would she ever again underestimate their ability to blunder into solutions. The moment the duo comingled their blood Brenna knew they had her. Bound in crackling tendrils of blue lightning, she could do nothing but shield herself from yet a third exile in limbo.

When her powers exploded against those of her adversaries, the blast threw Brenna down a long, dark corridor. She landed on hard earth, gasping as the force knocked the breath from her lungs. Lying on her back, staring up at the canopy of night stars, Brenna slowly became aware of a cold hollowness at the center of her being.

Humanity.

Mortality.

The screams of anger and frustration that rose in her throat sent the forest animals retreating into the shadows. Only when her voice broke against the parched walls of her throat did Brenna curl into a ball on her side and fall silent. There she stayed for the remainder of that night, and until the sun went down the next day.

There was no sleep. Brenna focused her thoughts inward, going into the deepest recesses of her mind in search of any surviving remnant of her power, any glowing ember she could nurse back to life. For centuries her power had been her companion and her consolation. Now, she found nothing but thin echoes of memory.

She was alone. Vulnerable. Frightened. But even as those alien, foul emotions clouded her thoughts, Brenna's own practical strength fought back. If she had attained her power once, she could do it again. In the meantime, how would she live? On what resources would she draw? What was her next move?

As the sun moved behind the mountains, Brenna summoned every degree of mental focus she retained and sent a single cry out into the Universe. Long moments passed. Sweat formed on her brow and her breathing grew labored. Then, the air around her stirred and a voice said, "Oh my, Brenna, this is a bit of a pickle, isn't it?"

She opened her eyes and looked up at Irenaeus Chesterfield. "You heard me," she said.

"Yes," he said, leaning against a boulder across from her, "I heard you."

Gritting her teeth against the weakness of the question, she asked, "How?"

The wizard regarded her speculatively and allowed his own arrogant mask to slide away. "How long has it been since you were last human?" he asked with surprising gentleness.

Brenna swallowed hard against the lump that rose in her

throat. "Hundreds of years. Not since I was a girl used cruelly by my father and brothers."

Irenaeus nodded. "What did you do to them?" he asked quietly.

"Ensured they died slowly and in screaming agony."

"Good," he said simply.

Brenna regarded him speculatively. "Irenaeus," she said, "are you being sensitive?"

He chuckled. "I will deny any such thing should you say that outside of this forest."

"Why did you seek your powers?" she asked.

Meeting her eyes, he replied, "Women were not the only ones used cruelly in the world into which we were born."

Silent seconds passed between them and then Irenaeus spoke again. "I can only imagine that you are feeling quite vulnerable right now, and, frankly, this does rather set back our plans."

The switch back to business seemed to clear Brenna's mind. She slowly rose to her feet and regarded him across the clearing. "Then rather than tolerate a setback," she said, "I suggest you fix this situation."

Irenaeus shook his head. "My dear," he said ruefully, "you over-estimate me. If I could perform *Veneficus Trajectio* we would have no need to operate in the shadows hiding from that do-gooder Barnaby Shevington."

"Are you telling me you can't do anything to help me?"

"I'm not saying any such thing," he said, "but you are going to have to make certain short-term accommodations."

"Like what?" Brenna asked suspiciously.

"Until we can reverse these unfortunate circumstances," Irenaeus said, "you will have to learn to use artifact-based magic, but to do so, you must regain your usual . . . confidence. I cannot have you feeling as you do now or you will be of no use to me."

Brenna regarded him critically. "Is that a threat?"

He smiled tolerantly. "I am wounded, my dear," he said. "I would hardly threaten a colleague facing a reversal of fortune. However, as a businessman speaking with my partner, we do have to be practical, now, don't we? Are you prepared to be an asset in this endeavor?"

Brenna regarded him coldly. "Do not worry about my *confidence*, Irenaeus," she said. "Provide me with the necessary tools and all will be well."

"Very well," he said, moving toward her as he reached into his pocket and drew out an amulet on a silver chain.

"I see you came prepared," Brenna said. "May I?"

"By all means," Irenaeus said, holding the necklace out to her. "Take it."

Brenna cautiously accepted the amulet, her eyes widening as she cradled the deep golden stone in the palm of her hand. "What is it?"

"Amber," he said, "the blood of the Mother Tree solidified around a feather of the Great Phoenix."

"The bird that arose from the ashes," she whispered.

"Encased in a stone of protection, regeneration, and immortality," he said. "Put it on."

Undoing the clasp, Brenna fastened the amulet around her neck.

"Wear it against your skin," Irenaeus instructed.

Brenna dropped the stone under the fabric of her blouse, resting her hand over it through the thin fabric. "It's vibrating," she said.

"Good," he said. "The stone is finding and assimilating the residue of the magic remaining in the cells of your body. That is an excellent sign. Try something simple."

Glancing around, Brenna spied a small pile of leaves and debris. She held out her hand, the fingers trembling slightly, and willed the material to rise into the air. As the leaves and twigs obeyed, confidence surged back into the fiber of Brenna's being. She flicked her fingers left and right, separating the material into three floating groups, then sending them into a slow rotating dance.

Irenaeus clapped his hands. "Excellent. We reached you in time. It may feel a bit clumsy in the beginning, but so long as you wear the amulet, you will be able to draw on at least a fraction of your former abilities."

"I am deeply in your debt, Irenaeus," she said.

"A debt I assure you that you will have ample opportunity to pay," he said. "Now, I believe you are investigating a real estate acquisition on the square in Briar Hollow, correct?"

She nodded. "I am," Brenna said, "but if I take up residence, the aos sí will know I am there."

Irenaeus clucked his tongue. "Yet again you make the mistake of underestimating me," he said. "My dear, I am the world's foremost dealer in black market metaphysical antiquities. Do you think I cannot supply you with adequate shielding from that Celtic annoyance? Close the deal."

"Very well," she said. "In the meantime, I will return to my temporary quarters."

"Ah, yes, the pizza man's establishment," Irenaeus said, "a quaint cover. May I offer you transportation? I'm afraid the amulet is not powerful enough to allow for your former transportation abilities. You may want to investigate learning to drive. Personally, I find the human's motor vehicle devices quite charming."

A frisson of annoyed impatience shot through Brenna, but she swallowed the reaction. "Thank you, Irenaeus," she said, clasping his fingers. "I'll look into that. And thank you for the amulet. I will not let you down."

"Oh, my dear," he said, "I know you won't. You have far more to lose than I do, now, don't you?"

With a twirl of his free hand, a cloud of energy formed around them and then the clearing was empty. The debris Brenna had sent dancing into the air minutes before quietly settled back to earth and all was still again.

16

The Alchemist's Workshop, Shevington

"Is Brenna Sinclair's return the path to nigredo for Jinx?" Myrtle asked, as Moira closed and bolted the heavy wooden door of her inner workshop.

The aos sí and the alchemist crossed the flagstones and ascended six steps to the raised area under the massive bay windows. The latticed panes towered over their heads, reaching toward the vaulted ceiling. Moira sat down behind her cluttered desk and pushed aside a heavy treatise entitled *Merculture: Myths and Merits* by C. S. K. Thunnus.

Myrtle regarded the book with a raised eyebrow. "Studying the sea folk?" she asked.

Moira sighed. "Many of their kind would like to seek sanctuary here in Shevington, but we lack proper access to the ocean. I am attempting to understand their culture more fully to determine if an artificial saltwater environment could be constructed in the upper valley."

"What is the source of their discord?" Myrtle asked.

"The growing decimation of their environment by the

detritus human society throws into the waters," Moira said tiredly. "It is a significant problem, along with the warming of the planet. We have been successful in getting a few undercover Druids into the National Oceanographic Institute. Their effectiveness is hampered by many factors, but at least it allows us to better monitor the situation."

Myrtle leaned back against the high-backed chair opposite the desk and sighed. "Do not despair, Moira," she said, "'Gaia is strong. Nature always finds a way."

"Tell that to the dinosaurs," Moira said. "Which raises another point. What was Barnaby thinking accepting the remaining plesiosaurs? They were perfectly happy in Scotland."

Myrtle cleared her throat. "Perhaps we could set aside matters of wildlife management for the moment and return to my original question about nigredo?"

Moira shivered as if she found the room cold. Absent-mindedly she pointed to the fireplace and muttered, "*Incendo.*"

A cheerful blaze sprang to life. With deft movements of her fingers, Moira sent the poker aloft and used it to carefully rearrange the fire, all without leaving her chair.

As the tool settled back into the stand on the hearth, Myrtle asked in a bemused tone, "Did you feel I needed a visual representation of the blackening?"

Moira laughed. "No," she said, "I just wanted the room warmer. I've been expending a great deal of energy these past days. It exacts a toll."

"You are working too hard," Myrtle said quietly. "You must take better care of yourself if you are to train Tori."

"Unlike you, aos sí," Moira said, "I am not immortal, simply extremely old. Which is the point of having a young apprentice. I like Tori. Her inner fire burns as brightly as her mother's." Then, as an afterthought, she added, "How I have missed Gemma."

"Moira," Myrtle said with soft insistence, "you are avoiding my question."

The other woman sighed. "Had Brenna not returned, I would have said Jinx had already completed the nigredo, but now I am not so sure. Do you recall what the human psychologist, Jung, said about nigredo?"

"Refresh my memory."

"To paraphrase his understanding of our alchemical process," Moira said, "he contended that the nigredo, the first stage, could only be completed when a new equilibrium was in place relative to the creation of the self."

"Jinx's complete acceptance of her role in the magical world," Myrtle observed quietly.

"Precisely," Moira said. "The very thing which led her mother flee."

Without hesitation, Myrtle said, "Jinx is stronger than Kelly. Fiona is right about that."

"That may be true, but at the moment of her testing, of her confrontation with despair, Kelly fled," Moira said. "I am not sure Jinx has yet been tested in that way. She was forced to face the consequences of her magic over the incident in the cemetery, and she subdued her panic when she learned about Shevington and what it entails, but a true test that compels the individuation? I don't think that has happened."

"She risked her life for the souls of those murdered girls," Myrtle said. "She confronted Brenna when Alexander and Knasgowa set her to the task."

Moira nodded. "Yes, she did, but we cannot begin to help her achieve the next stage, albedo, until we are certain. She is our last remaining hope, Myrtle. If she does not assume the mantle of authority here in Shevington, who will?"

Myrtle gazed out the window across the green fields of the valley. The sun was going down and lights had begun to twinkle in the windows of the farmhouses. "We could speak of Conner."

"We could," Moira said firmly, "but we won't."

MEANWHILE, back at the inn

WHEN MYRTLE TOLD Darby to pack our things, she must have anticipated the dinner with Barnaby. I was pleased, but not surprised, to find my favorite summer dress and matching light cardigan neatly rolled in a packing cube in my bag. When I shook out the dress, there wasn't a single wrinkle. I don't know if that was because of the theory about rolling clothes when you travel being right, or simply the effect of having a Fae in charge of my packing.

Regardless, I was grateful. While I was sure Barnaby and Moira had important things to say to us, I also had a date with Chase later that night. Magical alternate time streams or not, a girl has to keep her priorities straight.

Tori came out of her room dressed in a nice pair of jeans and a purple sweater. She grinned at me. "We both clean up good, girl."

"We better get a move on," I said, "before Amity has a hissy fit. Where's Rodney?"

A sound from the table caught my attention and I turned to find our already black-and-white rodent friend sporting a white dinner jacket worthy of Sinatra. I let out a low whistle. "Well," I said, "look at you!"

Rodney preened for us and then gave us the "well, who's giving me a lift" look.

Tori held out her hand. "She already has a date," she said, nodding at me, "so I'm claiming you, Double O Rodent."

Raising one paw, Rodney smoothed back the fur on his head with suave aplomb. Tori and I both laughed, and Rodney joined us with a toothy grin as he took his place on Tori's shoulder.

We went down to the lobby and found Amity caught up in a vigorous debate with Mrs. McElroy about the relative merits of organic wolf's bane over that raised with commercial fertilizer.

As we entered the room, Mrs. M. declared firmly, "All I'm saying is that anything in the way of miracles going on during the werewolf plagues of the 15th century didn't involve mixing up green powder. So, if it's all the same to you, I'll be growing my wolf's bane the natural way."

Amity sniffed, clearly offended. "You'll never get maximum yield that way."

"Well, Amity, darling," Mrs. M. said placidly, "maybe your livestock just doesn't shat enough."

Tori and I grinned at each other. I cleared my throat. "We're ready, Amity. Sorry to make you wait."

"Not at all," Amity said. "I've just been enjoying the most *earthy* conversation with Hester."

Mrs. M. smiled serenely. "My pleasure as always, Amity. Now off to your dinner with himself, the Mayor," she said. "The door'll be open whenever you get around to coming in."

We followed Amity out onto the square. It was just a few steps to the mayor's residence. Barnaby himself greeted us and we followed him into a warm parlor. Aunt Fiona, Chase, Myrtle, and Moira were already waiting for us. Chase instantly sprang to his feet. "Hi," he said, "you look really nice."

He paused for a beat and then added hastily, "Both of you."

Tori started to give him a hard time, but I caught her eye and shook my head imperceptibly. The last couple of days had been tough enough on Chase -- and I'd noticed Festus wasn't with him, which could only mean Chase hadn't been successful in dragging his father out of The Dirty Claw.

"How are your rooms at the Inn?" Barnaby asked, moving to stand in front of the fire. "I made Hester promise to give you the best she has and was informed that *all* of her rooms are the best."

"The rooms are lovely," I said. "Everything here is. We can't wait to see more of the city."

"Starting with my new house," Aunt Fiona gushed happily. "You're just going to love it. Oh! I know! You girls and Amity come for breakfast in the morning. We'll eat in my garden. I'll show you where I live when we go see the unicorns."

That touched off a round of questions from Tori directed at Moira about magical creatures, with Aunt Fiona and Amity joining in. Who knew my aunt had a thing for a Scottish shape-shifting, water horse critter called a kelpie?

When Barnaby excused himself to check on dinner, Chase came over and sat down beside me. "Hi," he said again, smiling.

"Hi, yourself," I answered, returning his smile. "I'm looking forward to our walk. Are we really going to climb up on the wall?"

"Yes," he said, "but using very civilized stone steps."

"Is there something special up there?" I asked.

He gave me a cryptic grin. "Guess you'll just have to wait and see."

Before I could press for more details, Barnaby called out from the doorway, "Shall we move to the dining room?"

Everyone got up and followed him down a paneled hallway to a room straight out of Buckingham Palace. After he took his place at the head of the table and we all pulled back our own chairs, there was easily room for another 20 or so people. But there was also another cozy (albeit enormous) fireplace, candles on the table, beautiful china bearing the Shevington family crest, and real silver heavy enough to be used as weaponry.

Then a crew of brownies began to carry in heaping platters

of food. My mouth instantly began to water and my stomach grumbled. I hadn't realized how hungry I was until I smelled the heavenly aromas. During the meal, we stuck to neutral but interesting topics. The conversation about magical creatures that had started in the other room carried over and segued into Barnaby regaling us all with tales of making friends with the local Sasquatch community for the first time.

"We hadn't been here in the New World more than a year or so when my people started coming to me with tales of seeing large, hairy, human-like creatures in the hills," Barnaby said. "Our new friends among the Cherokee assured me that my people were seeing Tsul 'Kalu."

"What's a Sool Kaloo?" I asked, reaching for more mashed potatoes.

"The literal translation is *sloping giant*," Moira replied, sipping from a goblet of red wine. "I'm ashamed to say that Fae or not, we took the stories as a tribal legend at first. It was rather xenophobic of us, actually."

"So this So Cool guy turned out to be Bigfoot?" Tori said, motioning to me to pass the potatoes her way.

Barnaby smiled. "Tsul 'Kalu," he corrected her, "and yes. One day a delegation from the local village walked right in the front gate of our then very crude settlement. I have to say they caused a bit of a panic until we discovered how quiet spoken and well mannered they are. Really a lovely race, although I admit they have some issues with their . . . fragrance."

"Isn't Bigfoot called the Skunk Ape down in Florida?" Tori asked.

Trust me. There's not a weird, unknown critter out there she hasn't heard about. Cryptozoology has always been one of her passions. Tori made me sit through every episode of *Monster Quest*, so this conversation had her completely in her element.

"Yes," Barnaby said, "that branch of the native Sasquatch population spends entirely too much time in the Everglades. I'm afraid getting wet does nothing to approve their olfactory presentation.

"He means they stink," Aunt Fiona supplied helpfully.

When everyone laughed, she added hastily, "But Barnaby is right. They're quite sweet. The Tsul 'Kalu who lives next door to me is ever so helpful. He's even better at getting things off shelves for me than you are, Chase."

"Well," Chase said, taking his turn with the circulating potatoes, "that's understandable, Fiona. If you're talking about Stan, he's 8 feet tall."

"*Stan*?" Tori and I said at the same time.

"It's short for Stanley," Fiona explained, as if we needed that useless clarification.

"I had that much figured out," I said. "But you really live next door to a *Bigfoot* named Stanley?"

My question seemed to confuse her completely. "Stanley is a perfectly nice name, dear," she said.

So not the point, but that's Shevington for you. If someone tells you they live next door to a big hairy ape (no offense intended to Stan), they actually do.

The conversation continued in the same light vein until we'd settled back in the front room with coffee and brandy. That's when Barnaby leaned back in his leather chair and got down to business. He looked at me directly, and said, "Well, Jinx, are you ready to find out why we've gone to such lengths to get you here with us tonight?"

Finally! Somebody who wasn't going to beat around the bush.

"I'd like that very much," I said. "I think everybody here will tell you I'm not big on surprises."

Barnaby smiled. "Myrtle has already shared that fact," he

said, "so, let me speak plainly. You're here because I'd like you take over my job."

Okay, he got points for not beating around the bush, but none of my friends seem to pay the slightest attention to what they're saying when I'm *swallowing*.

"Oh, dear," Barnaby said, quickly retrieving my cup before it hit the elegant Oriental carpet. "Are you alright?"

Still coughing, I held my hand up, waving it a little at the wrist to fend off all the hands suddenly reaching for me.

"I'm fine," I said. "Just swallowed wrong. Let me see if I heard you right. You want *me* to be the mayor of Shevington?"

Looking a little apologetic, Barnaby said, "Yes. I'm sorry if that was a bit abrupt, but there's really no reason not to just get to the heart of the matter. There's a great deal going on in the world of Fae politics and your services are needed."

"Why me?" I asked.

"In spite of your lack of training, your powers are stagger-ingly impressive."

"Okay," I said, trying not to sound as frustrated as I felt, "you all keep telling me that, but I have no idea what you're basing that on. I can talk to ghosts, float stuff around, have visions, but what's with this whole 'chosen one' thing?"

Barnaby looked at Myrtle and raised his eyebrows. "You haven't given her a practical demonstration?"

Myrtle shook her head. "No."

"May I ask why?" Barnaby said, beating me to the punch.

"Frankly," Myrtle said, "I, too, am unsure of the extent of her potential. I thought it best that we all get that information at the same time."

Barnaby turned to Moira. "Shall we use the Touchstone?" he asked.

"By all means," Moira said. Reaching under the neck of her

blouse, she drew out a heavy, black pendant on a gold chain. "We should start at the low end," she said.

To my surprise, Chase spoke up. "That would be me," he said as he reached for the pendant, placing the stone in the palm of his hand and closing his eyes. The stone began to glow with a soft, violet luminescence.

After a few seconds, Chase passed the stone to Amity. When she held it, the stone deepened to indigo. Aunt Fiona touched off a beautiful bluish hue.

Tori protested when Fiona held the stone out to her. "Me?" she said.

"Go ahead, dear," Aunt Fiona said. "You may be surprised."

Astonished might have been a better word. The stone immediately darkened to a deep, rich blue.

"May I have it, please?" Barnaby asked.

Tori passed it to him, and we all watched as the stone brightened to a glowing yellowish green. Barnaby returned the stone to Moira, who closed her eyes and concentrated as the color morphed to yellowish orange.

Then it was my turn. I accepted the stone, expecting it to go back to blue since that was the color my eyes turned the night in the cemetery with Brenna, but instead, the orange hue deepened slightly.

I don't claim to be any science nerd, but I did belong to a group called Rainbows in high school since Daddy is a Mason. Frowning at the stone in my hand, I said, "Isn't this backwards? I thought the color spectrum was red, orange, yellow, green, blue, indigo, and violet."

"In terms of frequency, you are correct," Moira said. "Violet light has the highest frequency and the shortest wavelength, but we are demonstrating the magical or alchemical spectrum. The most highly evolved alchemists move toward their powers in four stages -- nigredo, albedo, citrinitis, and rubedo. Red has the lowest frequency and the longest wavelength of the visible spectrum. I have studied for centuries to attain a level of power that registers orange with the stone. You can do it naturally."

The weight of her explanation hung in the air as I carefully handed the pendant back to Moira. It cooled to jet blackness again, and she slipped it around her neck and under the fabric of her blouse.

I looked at Barnaby. "Why now?" I asked.

"After centuries of separation, the Ruling Elders who represent the Old World Fae have reached out to me," he said. "They are interested in reuniting with us in common purpose. I have been asked to serve as ambassador to their court and to work as a participant in a conference to develop a unified body of governance. This is the most progress we've made toward codifying the Fae world since the Reformation. It's a significant step in the right direction, but I am not so foolish as to believe I will not be facing some degree of risk. I want to ensure that everything I've built here is securely guarded before I return to Europe to participate in these negotiations."

"Why can't Moira be mayor?" I asked.

Hey, I'm not a wimp or anything, but it never hurts to at least *ask* if there's a bigger boat available before you go after the shark.

The Alchemist shook her head. "I have no desire to be the governing officer of Shevington," she said. "My interests lie in the sciences of my kind. I am quite old, Jinx, and I wish to finish my magnum opus."

I frowned. "You're writing a big book?" I asked.

Moira laughed. "That is how the human world has corrupted the term" she said, "but an Alchemist's magnum opus is not a written work. In this life, we all engage in a personal journey. It has been described in many ways. For instance, you have heard of the quest for the Holy Grail?"

I wasn't about to tell her that my knowledge of the Holy Grail extended to Monty Python with a little splash of Indiana Jones, but I nodded.

"The story of the Grail, although the vessel does exist, is a way to describe the process of individuation that is part of personal growth," Moira went on. "For alchemists, this is paired with achieving the series of steps we've just described to you. They lead to the creation of a personal talisman of insight called the Philosopher's Stone."

"Isn't that supposed to turn any metal into gold?" Tori asked.

Moira nodded. "Yes," she said, "but not for the sake of acquiring the gold. The stone is for understanding the animus underlying all matter and purports to hold the powers of rejuvenation. That may mean that the stone can convey immortality, or simply be an instrument of tremendous healing. As no Alchemist has ever achieved this goal, I cannot say, but I wish to know. I want to devote myself to research, and, like Barnaby, I want my practical responsibilities here in the Valley to be transferred to someone of tremendous abilities. That is you, Tori."

The room fell silent. I think my crew was half expecting me to go running out again, but that wasn't going to happen.

Taking a deep breath, I said, "So, what would be involved in all of this? Are you asking us to move to Shevington?"

Barnaby shook his head. "No," he said. "Perhaps today on the street you noticed that many of our citizens were attired in clothing from your world?"

"Yes," I said, "I did notice. What's up with that?"

"Many of us pass back and forth from this time stream to yours," he said. "Some of us work in your world, or seek to make problems there better for humankind. One of the first things you need to understand about Shevington is that this is a place with an ethic of service, not just to our own kind, but also to this earth with which we have all been entrusted. Because the time streams move at different rates, you will be able to keep up your life in both. I could bore you to death with the appropriate algorithms, but a couple of hours or so away from your store is a day and more here. You may have a bit of our version of jet lag at first, but I like to think of it all as cramming a great deal more life into your allotted time. And I can promise you, Jinx, there is, as they say, never a dull moment in Shevington. The wildlife issues alone are enough to keep you more than sufficiently entertained."

I couldn't help laughing. "I've already had a little taste of that," I said. "Myrtle thinks I'm some kind of Dragonlet Whisperer or something."

"I heard about your encounter with the creatures," he said. "You have remarkable and untapped talents, Jinx, as we've tried to demonstrate to you here this evening. I have complete confidence that you will fully embrace your abilities and play a significant role in repairing the world of the Fae for the betterment of all the races of the earth. And, of course, Moira and I will be here to help you."

17

Barnaby Shevington was going to make one heck of a diplomat, because the next thing he said was that he knew I needed time to think about everything and to have a look around the city for myself. That was Chase's cue to stand and ask if I was ready to walk the wall. We excused ourselves and left the others talking about heading down to the stables.

When we stepped into the street, I was surprised to see that many of the stores were brightly lit and people were still coming and going with purpose.

"Shevington really isn't a town that ever stops," Chase explained as he offered me his arm. I tucked my hand in the crook of his elbow and we fell in step side by side.

"Why is that?" I asked.

"Many of the Fae don't need sleep," he said, "or if they do, it's just a few minutes here and there. Fae metabolic rates are all over the place. We werecats can keep going for hours and then just drop in place like big house cats and fall sound asleep."

"Good to know," I laughed. "Dare I ask where Festus is?"

Chase sighed. "At The Dirty Claw," he said. "I couldn't get

him to leave. Last time I saw him, he was sharpening his claws on the corner of the bar and talking about how this was the day he'd catch the red dot."

"You are not serious," I said. "Werecats play with laser pointers?"

It was Chase's turn to laugh. "Not exactly," he said. "Red Dot is a game we developed after laser pointers became the cat toy *de jour*. It's a drinking game involving pool balls. The players have to spot the red dot and swat the next ball -- in numerical order -- in the pocket before the dot disappears. If they fail, or miss the pocket, they have to take a drink of creamed whiskey."

"And if they make the shot?" I asked.

"They keep playing until they miss," he said.

"That sounds like a game that could go on forever," I said.

"Yes," he said, "except all the players get drunker by the round and the prize for winning is a nip cigar. So, sooner or later they're all drunk *and* high. The night usually ends with the whole crew of them flaked out on the pool table snoring."

"Okay," I said, "you do realize you're going to have to take me there, right?"

"God," he groaned, "I knew you were going to say that. Are you really sure you're ready to go to a werecat bar?"

"Dang straight I am," I declared. "So far the werecat bar is the coolest thing I've heard about in Shevington other than the unicorns. No way I'm missing a visit to The Dirty Claw."

"Oh," he said, "the unicorns have games of their own. Think of the place where dodge ball meets darts."

"Tori is gonna eat that up," I said. "She was a demon at dodge ball. She loved to torment all the prissy girls on the opposing team. It was the one place where we were guaranteed to get revenge on the cheerleaders."

"Now see," Chase said, "that is proof positive that girls are meaner than boys."

Before I could debate that point with him, we stopped at the bottom of a winding set of stone steps.

"We're here," Chase said.

"Here, where?" I asked looking around.

"The base of the wall," he said. "I wasn't kidding. We actually are going to take a walk around the top of the wall that borders the city. It's up these steps. Be prepared to be blown away."

I couldn't imagine how a wall was going to astound me in any way until we reached the top and I realized we'd been walking through a narrow, but beautiful park that encircles the city. Instead of the stone pathway I expected to find, we stood on a soft carpet of verdant grass. Trees grew on either side of the space, which was probably 12-15 feet wide. Tiny, sparkling lights adorned the branches and benches, raised flowerbeds, fountains, and burbling waterfalls sat staggered among the trunks. Some of the flowers glowed with soft fluorescence in the dim light. The scene was straight out of a storybook.

"Oh, Chase," I breathed. "This is incredible! Thank you so much for bringing me here."

"You like it?" he grinned happily. "It's one of my favorite places in the city."

"I can see why!" I said.

We began walking again, exchanging greetings with the people who passed us. The raised promenade wasn't crowded, and Chase seemed to be steering us toward a completely deserted section. We approached a rounded seating area that jutted out from the regular path.

"It's the top of a turret," Chase explained. "Come lean on the rail and let me show you something."

When I joined him, Chase pointed toward the mountains. "See?" he said. "That's the changing of the fairy guard. Those are the troops coming in from the Brown Mountain shift."

As I watched the approaching pinpricks of light, I realized

they were arranged in orderly ranks and files. "What does a fairy look like?" I asked. "It's kind of hard to imagine Tinkerbell on guard duty."

"Would you like to meet one?" Chase asked.

There's a silly question for you.

"Of course, I would," I said, "but how are you going to get their attention so far away?"

Chase removed a small flashlight from his pocket. He held it out over the rail and began to rhythmically click the switch on and off. It took me a few seconds to realize what he was doing.

"Are you sending Morse code?" I asked.

"Yes," he said, "it comes in handy when you're patrolling in the mountains."

Before I could ask him how a werecat managed to carry a flashlight, a tiny bolt of vibrant light shot straight toward us out of the gathering dusk, stopping just inches from Chase's nose.

"Chase McGregor, you old tomcat," the tiny being declared in a surprisingly deep baritone voice. "Have you actually gone and gotten yourself a girlfriend?"

"Much with the discretion there, Ironweed?" Chase growled, taking a playful swipe at the fairy, who executed a perfect somer-sault, ducking under Chase's arm and tapping him on the end of the nose.

"Whoa! Point to the little man with wings," the fairy declared heartily, "and the crowd goes wild."

"That's not fair," Chase grumbled, "you sucker punched me."

Clearing my throat, I said, "Now, now boys. Fight nice."

Remembering his manners, Chase said, "Jinx Hamilton, allow me to introduce Major Aspid Istra, Commander of the Brown Mountain Guard."

The fairy darted over to hover in front of me. He was about six-inches tall, wearing black commando fatigues complete with combat boots and a purple beret. The only thing that kept him from looking like any other Special Forces guy was the fact that two incandescent wings protruded from his shoulders, beating brightly in the circle of light surrounding his body.

As I watched, the Major swept off his beret, bowed, and said, "My friends call me Ironweed, and I hope you, pretty lady, will count yourself among them."

Even though it was a really bad line, I couldn't help myself. I giggled, which won me a rakish grin from Ironweed.

"Chase tells me this is your first visit to Shevington," the fairy said. "How are you liking it?"

I turned to Chase. "You got all of that into one Morse code message?" I asked.

"Oh," Ironweed said, "he said more than that. According to him . . . "

Chase took another cuff at the fairy. "That will be enough out of you," he warned. "She wanted to meet a fairy. She's met you. Now scram. Go do your duty or something."

Ironweed looked at me, held his tiny hand up to his ear in the shape of a telephone receiver, and mouthed, "Call me."

I mouthed back, "Will do."

And with that, he zoomed back into the night to rejoin his troops.

"Fairies," Chase grumbled, "bunch of blabber mouths."

Slipping my hand back in the crook of Chase's arm, I said, "So you told him I'm your girlfriend, huh?"

Sighing, Chase said, "What I said was that you're the very nice lady I'm dating and for once could he please be on his good behavior. Guess you can tell how well that worked."

"He's cute," I said, "and sort of bad-boy macho all at once. Are they all like that?"

"It's a fairy thing," Chase said. "Don't ever get drunk with them. They'll put you under the table."

We stood there in silence for a few seconds, and then I said, softly, "You've been the soul of patience since I ran out of the basement."

"After how much I screwed everything up," he said, "I didn't think I had any right demanding anything of you."

I turned toward him. "You didn't screw everything up," I said. "You were scared to tell me the truth about yourself, just like I was scared to tell you I'm a witch."

He nodded, and then said, "There's a little more to it, though, and I think you need to hear it from me."

Even though little alarm bells were going off in my head, I didn't take my eyes away from his face. "Okay," I said, "tell me."

After a slight hesitation, he said, "Not all of the Fae races are ... genetically ... compatible."

Okay. Bigger leap than I thought.

"What do you mean 'genetically compatible'?"

Even in the dim glow, I could see the flush on his cheeks. The fact that Chase can blush at the drop of a hat is one of the things I love most about him.

"There's no law against marriage of any kind," he said, stammering a little, "but some couples can't have . . . there's a risk with hybridiz ... not all DNA ... "

Thankfully, the light dawned on me before he choked on his own words.

"Are you trying to tell me that werecats and witches can't have children together?" I asked.

"No one knows for sure," he said quietly, "but other pairings haven't worked out well, so there's a tradition that werecats only marry werecats."

I took a minute to digest this new information. "We're kind of not at the stage of talking about children," I finally pointed out.

He caught hold of my hands. "No," he said, "but what if we were?"

What if we were?

For the record, I'm not a huge fan of hypotheticals. In general life gives you enough actual problems. No need to create your own custom mash up.

Chase was watching me closely. In the moonlight, I could see the hope in his eyes . . . and the love.

"If we were," I said, "we'd get the best advice we could and then make a decision together."

He couldn't keep from asking the question directly. "You'd give up the chance to have kids to be with me?" he said.

To be real honest with you, I liked the idea of raising a child with Chase, but I wasn't hung up on the whole DNA thing.

"You've seen my family tree," I said. "Surely you can understand why I'm totally good with adopting."

Chase tried to stifle a giggle, but it didn't work. Then I got tickled, and then we were both laughing so hard we were crying.

"Can you imagine Festus kitten-sitting?" he gasped. "We'd come home and find the litter stoned and shooting craps in the living room while Grandpa watched cat videos on National Geographic. He has his own copy of *Mating Habits of Jungle Cats*."

"Stop," I begged, "I can't breathe."

Chase patted me on the back. Then somehow I was in his arms, and I couldn't breathe for an entirely different reason.

When we did come up for air, I rested my head against his chest. I fit just under his chin.

"I like Shevington," I whispered, "and I love you."

"I love you, too," he said, tightening his hold on me.

Under my ear, a deep contented thrumming rose in volume.

Chase was purring, and it was the most wonderful sound I'd ever heard.

18

On the square in Briar Hollow

The old man in the John Deere tractor cap stared at the dark store windows. He'd knocked back so much of that expensive swill those little gals called coffee he wouldn't sleep for a week, which was good. He had a job to do, and he'd like to get finished in time to get home for the 10 o'clock news.

When Brenna Sinclair first approached him, Joseph "Fish" Pike, was sure he'd said no. But then he looked at the clock on the wall and realized he'd been talking to the woman for more than an hour. She was sitting right there in the parlor on Martha Louise's good sofa, and danged if Fish wasn't blabbing about how nice it was to be talking to a lady again now that his wife was gone.

And Brenna knew things about him she couldn't know, like how his grandpappy turned into a panther by the light of the moon. Nobody else ever believed Fish when he told that story, so he couldn't imagine how Brenna found out. Fish hadn't tried to talk about any of that for a long time because he didn't like it when folks treated him like a crazy old man. But he knew what he saw when he was just 8 years old. Grandpa Jeremiah Pike turned into a mountain lion right there in front of the farmhouse.

When Fish told his daddy about what he saw, Fish got a slap for his troubles. "What your grandpappy does with those high and mighty McGregors is none of your business, boy. Don't you never say another word about it," his daddy snarled. Rubbing the red mark on his face, Fish wasn't about to ask again.

But that didn't keep him from hiding in the shadows still as a mouse and listening when the grownups talked. Not too many weeks passed before Fish had put some of the story together. What his daddy was really mad about was that grandmammy couldn't turn into a mountain lion, which somehow meant her son couldn't either. Unless daddy could turn into a painter, he couldn't go to someplace called "The Valley" with grandpappy.

As Fish got older, he started noticing other things, like them lights up around Brown Mountain and signs of the Little People the old Cherokees talked about. He knew there was more going on up in the hollers than people let on, but he never could get it all straight and finally he just quit talking about such as that. There was work to do and a family to raise. Stories of haints and spooks were just something to scare the young'uns and keep 'em in bed at night where they belonged.

Then Miss Brenna Sinclair sat there on the good parlor sofa and told him how Chase McGregor's people and that old busybody Fiona Ryan had stolen his heritage from him. But Miss Brenna said she could set it all right and promised to take Fish to The Valley if he'd just get into the store that night and put something down in the basement for her.

It wasn't that Fish thought there was anything up in that so-called valley that would be of any use to him, he just wanted to go up there because his daddy couldn't. The idea of getting something over on that mean old varmint even though he was long dead and in his grave appealed to Fish.

As for breaking into the store, that wouldn't be hard. Fish had jimmied many a lock in his day, but he cackled with laughter when Breanna handed him an old dirty canvas miner's cap with a leather brim. It was missing its light, but the bracket was there.

"This is what you want me to put down in the basement?" he asked. "What in the Sam Hill for?"

She fixed him with an icy glare and Fish felt the hairs on the back of his scrawny neck stand straight up.

"Our dealings will be ever so much more pleasant, Mr. Pike, if you don't ask impertinent questions," she said. "I trust I won't have to repeat myself on that point?"

The stutter that had disappeared from his speech when he was a gangly teen crept back into Fish's respond. 'N-n-n-n-n-no, m-m-m-m-m-m'am."

"Good," she said. "I knew you would see the wisdom of my suggestion."

So there he was, two nights later, skulking around in the dark, unaware that across the square, Brenna, safely hidden in the confines of the old hardware store, was, at that very moment, unlocking the door to her own basement and descending into the darkness below.

She chose to purchase the building on the advice of the late, insufferable Howard McAlpin. In 1908, eleven years before a federal statute was passed making Prohibition the law of the land, the state of North Carolina outlawed the sale of alcoholic beverages. For their troubles, the pious legislators did little more than ensure the guaranteed profitability of illegal liquor manu-facturing, popularly known as "bootlegging."

In Briar Hollow, the primary beneficiary of such activity was the Sheriff himself, Cletus Adams. In order to hide his illegal side-business, and to facilitate his operations, Adams had a tunnel dug from the basement of the courthouse to the basement of the hardware store, the site of a covert drinking club or "speakeasy."

When Brenna purchased the store, she found the tunnel intact, barred on the courthouse end by nothing more than a locked door. This access not only allowed her to move about the building at night and confer with McAlpin, but it also put Brenna in a direct line with the fairy mound, the target of the plan Irenaeus had so carefully crafted.

While Fish Pike studied the store windows and worked up the courage to commit an act of breaking and entering, Brenna moved carefully, but swiftly through the long abandoned passageway, holding the old miner's lamp in her hands. Although she would never have admitted it, her own initial reaction to the relic had been as disparaging as Mr. Pike's. That is, until Irenaeus explained the story behind the object.

The cap belonged to a member of a "sand hog" construction crew responsible for excavating the maze of tunnels beneath New York City in the 19th century. When a section of roof collapsed on him, the man's panic and will to live burned so brightly that the energy infused the lamp, sending a searing glow through the debris. To the amazement and relief of the trapped man, an escape route opened before him, which allowed him to clamber to safety.

Now, when the pieces of the cap were separated, nothing but simply lighting the lamp was required to rekindle the energy of the miner's desperation. If Fish Pike placed the cap in the store basement as directed, and Brenna lit the lamp in the courthouse, a new tunnel would open in a perfect line between them to reunite the two halves of the object.

Rather than risk a direct confrontation with the aos sí, Irenaeus had put some sort of surveillance system in place inside the shop. Earlier in the evening, he contacted Brenna to tell her the building was empty, and she dispatched the ever-willing Mr. Pike. Now, she had only to wait for the new cellular telephone in the pocket of her cloak to receive a message from Pike, and she would light the lamp.

While she waited, above her at street level, Fish Pike finally decided to make his move. He crept quietly down the alley, keeping to the shadows, and being careful not to trip over his own feet or run headlong into a trash can. When he reached the back of the shop, he was surprised to see the Hamilton girl's red Prius parked under the newly erected carport.

Miss Brenna had assured him the building would be empty. Pike stood in the shadows for a minute, chewing at his lower lip. If he broke in and got caught, he'd have to face the law. If he didn't break in, he'd have to face Brenna. Weighed in that light, dealing with the sheriff was a much better option than a redheaded woman who already scared the daylights out of Fish. Time to get at it.

After putting his ear to the door and listening for any sound of activity inside, Fish removed a thin metal tool from his pocket, squinted at the lock, and deftly released the mechanism with a simple twist of his wrist. He stepped through the opening and quickly closed the door behind him, letting his eyes adjust to the dim light.

Earlier that day, as he'd played chess with that imbecile Homer Ford, Fish had carefully mapped out the lay of the ground floor. He knew that the door to his immediate left opened into the apartment where the girl, Tori, lived. The second door on the right led to the basement.

What Brenna wanted him to do didn't make any sense, but Fish knew better than to say so. He was supposed to go down to the basement, put the cap on the floor right in front of the steps, and then just hit one button on the cell phone she'd insisted he carry with him.

Fish didn't have the slightest idea how to use one of the danged things, so Brenna put in her own message and told him he only had to hit the button marked "Send." Once he did that, she said he could leave.

Accomplishing all of that didn't take 10 minutes, but on his way out the back of the store, Fish could have sworn something flew right by his head. He heard 3 little taps, followed by eight more in a pattern that triggered vague recognition in his head.

Pausing with one foot over the threshold, he tapped the pattern on the doorframe, humming to himself, "I saw the light, I saw the light." Now what in tarnation would put Hank Williams on his brain?

Shaking his head at his own foolishness, Fish closed and locked the door behind himself and went home.

Had he lingered a little longer, he might have felt the building shudder as Brenna Sinclair lit the miner's lamp in her hand. As she watched, a large circle began to revolve on the brick wall in front of her as if an unseen hand scrubbed away at the surface with a rough cloth. With each rotation, the circle deepened, moving through the foundation and into the earth beyond.

Brenna stepped into the opening, moving forward slowly with the lamp held out before her. She had expected something more spectacular than this gradual etching process, but she could not deny the inexorable progress no matter how tedious the pace. Finally, the foundation of a second structure appeared, and then the back of another brick wall. Without warning, the lamp flew from her hand, settling itself into the bracket attached to the filthy cap lying on the basement floor.

The reflector, which was turned toward the ceiling, cast a dull glow around the cavernous space. There was just enough light for Brenna to see that she was not standing in the magical archive Irenaeus described. This was nothing but a filthy, cluttered basement full of skittering spiders and old cardboard boxes collapsing into themselves.

Brenna felt anger and frustration boil up inside her. After all she had done, all she had survived, had she really come back to the place where she could once again be made the victim of a scheming man's lies? She didn't know what game Irenaeus Chesterfield was playing, but she intended to find out and end it.

Brenna turned on her heel, intent on stalking back to the hardware store, when the sound of voices made her stop. At first she thought Jinx and Tori had returned, but these women sounded older and more . . . tentative.

The doorknob above her on the rickety landing jiggled slightly and then the door creaked open. Curious, Brenna shrank into the shadows and waited.

19

C hase and I stayed in our secluded spot on the wall
until the lights of the Brown Mountain Guard receded
into the darkness. "Where do they go?" I asked, my
head still resting against his chest.

"The Fairy Barracks are on the far side of the city," he said.
"We'll walk over there tomorrow so you can watch their aerial
drills."

"That must be like watching dragonflies flying in formation,"
I said.

He laughed. I liked the sound under my ear. "A fairy can out-
maneuver a dragonfly any day of the week," he said, "and if you
don't believe it, ask a fairy. The only thing they like more than
flying is bragging."

Leaning back a little, I gave him an evil grin.

"Uh oh," he said warily. "What's that look for?"

"Well," I said, "now that you've mentioned bragging, how
about you take me to The Dirty Claw?"

When his expression wilted a little around the edges, my
grin expanded. "You thought I was going to forget about the bar,
didn't you?"

"I *hoped* you were going to forget," he said. "Just remember, this was your idea."

We turned around and went back in the direction we'd come. When we passed the stone staircase, Chase explained that we were behind the main business district and were heading toward the city's main entrance.

"When we get to the front gate," he said, "we'll go back down to street level. The bar is about two blocks down to the right."

Even if you didn't know that The Dirty Claw is a werecat bar, anyone within a one-block radius could figure it out pretty quick from the singing alone. Or yowling, depending on how you choose to interpret the sound. As we got closer, I was shocked to hear lyrics I recognized.

"Isn't that 'Stray Cat Strut?'" I asked.

Chase groaned. "Oh," he said, "that is *not* a good sign. If they break into the score from *Cats*, you can bet the whole place is stoned to the gills on nip."

Laughing, I said, "You make the place sound like some kind of opium den."

He shot me a sideways look. "Tell me how well that description fits after you see the hookah pipes in the back lounge."

"You mean like the caterpillar smoked in *Alice in Wonderland*?" I asked incredulously.

"Note the role of the Cheshire *Cat* in that story," Chase pointed out sardonically.

Suppressing a giggle, I followed him down the street toward the raucous voices. From the outside, The Dirty Claw looks like any perfectly respectable pub. When we stepped into the vestibule, however, a huge framed photo of a seductive-looking lady Persian bearing the autograph, "To Snooky Paws with love, Fluffy Lamour," greeted me.

I turned to Chase. "Fluffy *Lamour*?"

"Uh, yeah," he said, "she was kind of a big deal back in the

Forties. You may have heard of her sister, the actress, Dorothy . . ."

"Stop!" I commanded. "I don't think I'm ready to play a round of 'out that werecat.'"

Chase held the door open for me and we stepped into a scene straight out of *Animal House*, except the frat brothers were actual animals. A thin-looking black leopard with a cigarette dangling from his mouth sat at the piano pounding out the driving beat of the music accompanied by a bored looking lion on bass, and cheetah in shades playing a sax.

Shouting a little to be heard over the din, I said, "I thought all the werecats were mountain lions."

Leaning down to speak in my ear, Chase replied, "Just the ones from North Carolina. People come and go from all over the world in Shevington. About the only thing you can count on is that the big cats are still working and the house cats are all retired and living the good life. That's Dad's bunch over by the pool table."

He pointed toward the back of the bar where I saw a gang of about half a dozen house cats on top of a pool table engaged in a rousing game of what I assumed was Red Dot. A remote controlled laser pointer suspended from the ceiling randomly shot a burst of light into pockets on the table as contestants lurched over the felt and attempted to bat the next designated ball into the pocket.

Festus was lounging on the far corner of the table beside a line of empty shot glasses.

"It doesn't look like he's winning," I said.

"Big surprise there," Chase answered, taking me by the elbow. "Come on, let's go hear his excuse for missing dinner with the Lord High Mayor."

As we approached, Festus narrowed his eyes as if he was

trying to focus on us. Then he jumped up and yelled, "Chase, my boy! Get furry and join the game."

Blushing a little, Chase, said, "Thanks, Dad, but I'll pass. Hey guys, this is my friend Jinx. Jinx, that's . . . "

As he made the introductions, I tried to place fur and faces to names.

Leo was a large black and white domestic shorthair with a notch in his left ear engaged in a half-hearted game of patty cake with Maurice, a cross-eyed Siamese who kept missing his opponent's paws. A Cornish Rex wearing a cable knit sweater barely looked up when Chase called his name.

"That's Aloysius," Chase said. "He's the reigning Red Dot champ. Nothing shatters his focus."

That left Merle, Earl, and Furl, three Scottish Fold littermates who waved at me in happy triplicate. From their glassy eyes and the globs of ropey drool on their chins, I could tell they'd all been enjoying their fair share of mood-altering kitty weed.

I tugged at Chase's sleeve. When he leaned down, I whispered, "This might be kind of a personal question, but do all of you have distinct breeds?"

"Every werecat can assume large and small forms," he said. "As big cats, Merle, Earl, and Furl are mountain lions like me and Dad."

"So, uh . . . when you're not . . . do you . . . " I faltered and fell silent.

"Are you asking me if I'm a scruffy yellow tomcat like Dad?" Chase asked, his eyes twinkling.

"Uh, sort of," I nodded, embarrassed.

"No," he said, "in my small form I'm a Russian Blue."

"Really?" I said, my voice going a little breathy.

Interest kindled in Chase's eyes. "Yeah, why?" he asked.

Now I had backed myself completely into a corner. "I, uh, sort of have a thing for gray cats," I admitted sheepishly.

Chase snaked his arm around my waist. "Well, I certainly hope so," he said rakishly.

That won him a punch in the arm as we settled down on barstools to watch the next round of Red Dot. Chase got the bartender's attention. He was a burly Canadian Lynx with forepaws like hams. The tufts on his ears swiveled in our direction as Chase ordered two bottles of Litter Box Lager.

"Not the best name for a beer," I said. "Please tell me it doesn't taste like something that belongs *in* the litter box."

"It doesn't," Chase assured me. "They carry a beer called Ye Olde Cat Pi ... er, by-product. Trust me. Don't order it."

Do I even need to tell you how much fun I was having by this time?

Turning my attention back to the pool table, I could see that Aloysius really was the only serious player, expertly swatting balls into the pockets with feline grace. Every time he won a nip cigar, he simply flicked it toward one of his cronies and went back to work.

"Is he always so focused?" I asked Chase.

"I think it keeps him warm," Chase said. "Hairless cats always seem to be wound kind of tight."

"What's the story on Leo's ear?" I asked.

Chase snickered. "His second wife caught him making time with a South American Jaguar named Lupita and dang near ripped it off. Maurice is his best friend. Leo has to keep him from walking into walls -- literally."

Just then, Aloysius missed a shot, arching his back and hissing in irritation, which put Festus up for the next round of play. Rising unsteadily to a standing position, he wobbled forward on three legs, readied himself, and slurred, "Purrllll."

He meant "pull," which was the cue for the laser pointer to fire at a pocket.

Spotting his quarry, Festus spun on his one hind leg and actually got a front paw on the 9 ball before he did a faceplant on the felt.

"Whoa," Earl said, "steady there, old man."

Both he and Merle tried to lift Fesus, which led to all three of them going down as pool balls flew everywhere. Festus managed to raise his whiskers high enough off the table to call out, "I missed. Bring on the whiskey," at which point Chase slid off the barstool and said, "I don't think so, Dad."

Amid cries of "spoiled sport" and "'fraidy cat,'" Chase deftly extricated his father from the fur pile and tucked the protesting old codger under one arm.

"Put me down you no good worthless, hairball," Festus demanded. "I licked your fur when you were a kitten, you ungrateful alley cat."

Chase caught hold of Festus' front paws and held them in place. "That'll be enough out of you," he said sternly.

Festus regarded him with a blearily bobbling gaze. He started to argue, but the old guy just couldn't keep his eyes open. As we watched, his head dropped down on Chase's wrist, and he started to snore.

"Thank God," Chase said, looking at his Dad with loving tolerance, "he is so much easier to deal with when he passes out." Turning to me he added, "Do you mind? I need to get him home and tucked in bed."

I was laughing so hard tears were running down my cheeks. "Not at all," I said, "but you have to promise we can come back."

Shaking his head, Chase said ruefully, "Great, another party animal in the family."

We said our good-byes, weaving our way through the crowd with Festus still draped over Chase's arm snoring contentedly.

Once we were out in the street, Chase transferred his father to a more comfortable position and we walked slowly back to the Inn.

At the door, Chase said, "I guess this is where I say good night."

"Don't I get a good night kiss?" I teased.

"Right," he said, "as I cradle my drunken alley cat father in the crook of my arm."

Giggling, I stood on tiptoe and gave him a peck on the cheek. "You be sure he drinks plenty of water in the morning," I said. "Hangovers are worse when you're dehydrated."

"I'll tell him you said so," Chase said.

I watched the two of them walk away. At the corner, Chase turned and waved. I waved back and only went into the inn when he disappeared from sight.

20

Beau Longworth finished his materialization at the base of the Confederate monument. Nearby, a small gaggle of paranormal tourists talked excitedly, holding their camera screens out to one another to compare the images they had just captured. Beau was most grateful for Miss Tori's tutelage regarding the evolution of photography. He was aware of the ponderous equipment carried by Matthew Brady during what was now referred to as the "Civil War." Frankly, Beau still bristled a bit at that name. The conflict had been anything but civil.

At any rate, in those days, several pounds of accouterment were required to create a single, grainy sepia-toned photograph. In the 21st century, however, even laymen carried ubiquitous electronic boxes Miss Tori referred to as "smartphones."

Both the name and the multipurpose functionality of the devices appealed to the Colonel's utilitarian nature. As he understood the concept, telephones were a considerable improvement over the telegraphic method of his own day, but Beau did not completely grasp how the connection was established without wires. But the inclusion of a camera capable of creating high-quality color images to serve in tandem with the device was nothing less than a marvel.

Thus armed, all citizens were in a position to function as front-line journalists. Oddly enough, however, Miss Tori assured him that the power was not always used wisely. With what insight he held into the nature of humankind, the information did not surprise Beau, but it did disappoint him. The regression of social responsibility since his own former lifetime came as a cruel blow for a man who had always hewed to a belief in the perfectibility of human character.

Miss Tori had also kindly served as something of a paranormal acting coach for his appearances on the square. She explained that he must never give the ghost seekers conclusive proof of his existence. The goal was to continue to lure them to Briar Hollow in continual search of better evidence, thus leveraging their presence to spend dollars in support of the local economy.

She showed him numerous, highly debated spectral images. He chose to model his own materializations after the 1936 photograph of the Brown Lady of Raynham Hall in England. Although potentially a fake, Beau found the vaguely human form of the woman descending the stairs to be tastefully translucent and decidedly worthy of long-standing debate. After some practice in front of Miss Tori, the Colonel had perfected the correct amount of energy to project himself into an amorphous suggestion of his true self, which, judging from the reaction of tonight's assemblage, was garnering positive critical reviews.

Leaving the ghost hunters to their speculations, Beau crossed the street and passed unencumbered through the front door of the store. Although he had not wanted to pry, Jinx's tearful visit to the cemetery left Beau deeply concerned about the stresses with which she was dealing. After his materializations, however, he often visited the store, which created the perfect opportunity now for him to pay a call without appearing to be overly protective.

The fact that the first floor was dark and deserted did not bother him. The Colonel assumed that he would find Jinx and Tori in the basement with Myrtle, but to his surprise that area was deserted as well. He saw nothing that would give him cause for alarm and was about to return to the cemetery when he heard the door above him open and close quickly. The furtiveness of the sound struck Beau as odd. Dimming his energy to an even lower level than that he used for the tourists, Beau started to investigate, but stopped when the basement door gave a tentative creak.

As he watched, the transparent figure of a disheveled old man came down the steps holding a filthy canvas cap with a leather bill in his hands. At first Beau thought he was looking at another ghost like himself, but then he realized the man in front of him was in color, not the shaded gray tones of a disembodied spirit. Jinx had told Beau that there was some form of alternate reality in play in the basement. Could it be possible that he, himself, was standing in one dimension and the man with the cap was in another?

The elderly intruder came no farther than the last step, where he now stood nervously looking left and right. Seeming to assure himself that he was, indeed, alone, the man bent over and carefully deposited the cap on the floor. The instant the object left his hand, he turned on his heel and fled back upstairs. Beau heard his steps cross the floor and pause at the back door. An odd little series of taps echoed through the stillness, and then the door opened and closed again.

Before Beau could even begin to surmise why an interloper would break into the shop only to deposit a piece of odd headgear on the basement floor, he felt a breath of wind stir at his back. Turning, Beau watched as a thin, whirling cloud formed on the wall.

After a moment or two, a wavering opening became visible, and the red-haired sorceress, Brenna Sinclair, stepped through. But, like the old man before her, Brenna appeared to be only a projection of her true self. Beau instantly understood that she could not see the basement as he saw it any more than the elderly man possessed that perception. How long that would remain the case, Beau could not guess, but for the moment, it gave him a tactical advantage.

What the Colonel did know, with much greater certainty, was that Brenna Sinclair represented a danger to his friends. She had infiltrated their home. It was Beau's duty to locate Jinx and give her the information. But how?

He hurriedly looked around the area Miss Tori insisted on calling their "lair." Nothing seemed out of place with the exception of one or two volumes that had been taken from the book-case by the fireplace. Then, his eye fell on something lying just at the entrance to the long aisle that ran between the endless rows of shelves stretching so far into the distance they seemed to shrink in enveloping blackness.

Going down on his knee to get a closer look, Beau recognized one of the compressed food pellets Jinx insisted Master Rodney the Rat consume on a daily basis. Allowing his eye to roam over the floor, Beau spotted a second pellet a few feet away. He stood up and moved forward until he found the third and knew he was being presented with a trail to follow.

The Colonel glanced over his shoulder. He saw Brenna Sinclair raise her head as if she were listening to something, but he didn't have time to find out what. Levitating a few inches into the air, Beau floated down the aisle, following the trail of rat food. As he picked up speed, the rectangle of light behind him grew smaller and smaller.

Previously, Beau had formed no sense of the vastness of the subterranean archive through which he now traveled. He was surprised how many moments passed until he attained its farthest reaches and came to a halt hovering before a door. Reaching forward, he turned the knob, intent upon completing his mission, but found himself staring at a solid wall.

In life, the Colonel had not been a man given to a belief in the fantastical, but after more than two hundred years as a ghost and then having made the acquaintance of magical beings, his opinions had evolved considerably. There must be more to the portal before him than a simple plaster barrier. Perhaps a second latch concealed nearby?

Beau examined the adjacent wall and found nothing. Then, his gaze wandered over the storage boxes piled in the shelves behind him. To his surprise, he recognized the name on one of the labels: James McGregor -- the Masonic brother who found Beau's body on the battlefield, arranged his funeral, and contacted his wife and daughter to inform them of his demise.

Gliding over to the box, Beau lifted the lid. There, carefully folded and lying on top of the contents, he found McGregor's Masonic apron. Running his cold, lifeless fingers over the soft lambskin, Beau whispered, "If only you were here to help me, Brother McGregor."

From somewhere to his left, a voice said, "What service do you require, Brother Longworth?"

Pivoting toward the sound, Beau looked on the face of the man in whose debt he had remained since the day of his own death.

"Brother McGregor," he said, his words thick with emotion, "how can I ever thank you for the services you have already performed for me and mine?"

"Please," the other spirit said, "call me James. And any service performed was my great honor, sir."

Inclining his head in gracious acknowledgement, the Colonel replied, "The honor is mine. To my friends, I am Beau. I can think of no man I would more heartily wish to call friend than you, sir."

James offered his hand, and to Beau's immense relief, he was able to take it.

"Then so may it ever be," James said. "What brings you to the home of the aos sí?"

With as much brevity as he could muster, Beau explained the recent series of events and the significance of Brenna Sinclair's presence in the basement.

James listened intently, and then said, "The aos sí must be in Shevington, or this sorceress could not have advanced so far beyond the defenses that guard the fairy mound."

"I have only recently learned of this realm of Shevington," Beau said, "but I must warn my friends of the danger. Is there a way to access this other plain?"

James shook his head. "Not for ones such as us," he replied. "We are but shades of our mortal selves."

"There must be a way," Beau insisted. "We are both military men, sir. I am not yet ready to admit defeat."

By this time, they had both floated over to the door. James studied the portal for a moment and then said, as if suddenly struck by inspiration, "We buried you with your pocket watch, did we not, Beau?"

"You did," the Colonel replied. "Why?"

"Although I see the haunting aspect of the watch chain there on your vest," James said, "the object itself still exists in this stream of time, even if it does lie encased in your casket. Although I was in life but a mere dabbler in things alchemical, I believe that if you attempt to cast the watch through the entrance to Shevington, it will reform as whole matter on the other side. It is but the slightest of chances, but if your young friend were to see your watch, would she interpret it as a message?"

"She would," Beau said without hesitation. "Miss Jinx is a most remarkable woman. But, how do we move beyond the solid barrier presented by this wall?"

James smiled. "Due to the role my family has long played in the life of Shevington," he said, "I can, in that respect, be of assistance."

At that, he held his hand aloft and began to softly chant in a language Beau did not recognize. To his amazement, the plaster drew away until they were looking through the opening into a beautiful, sunlit mountain meadow.

"Is all of Shevington like that?" Beau asked, pointing toward the scene.

"Like that," James said, "and ever so much more. But please, make haste, I do not know how long I can hold the portal open."

Beau reached down and drew out his heavy pocket watch, unfastening the chain from his vest. "What are the chances that Miss Jinx will find this?" he asked.

"I do not know," James admitted, "but the entrances to The Valley are patrolled. Perhaps, at the very least, the watch will be taken to the Lord High Mayor."

Gathering the timepiece and chain in his hand, Beau lobbed them through the opening, but before they could hit the ground, a flash of iridescent blue careened across their view, snatching the watch in mid-air, and flying rapidly away.

"Damnation," James swore under his breath.

"What was that creature?" Beau asked.

"That," James said, "was a dragonlet and I fear, Brother Longworth, that our tenuous plan has now gone terribly awry."

21

F or what must have been the tenth time, Gemma cut her eyes over to the passenger side of the car. She just could make out Kelly's profile in the light from the dashboard.

"Kell, are you sure about this?" she asked. "We can still turn around."

Although Kelly Hamilton was normally soft spoken and the soul of good manners, her frayed nerves couldn't take much more. Telling Jinx and Tori the truth about what happened back in high school had been stressful enough, but now . . . No. She wasn't going to think about any of that. She just wanted to check on Jinx and get back home.

"For God's sake, Gemma," she snapped, "would I be sitting here in this car with you if I wasn't sure? This is *my* idea after all. I just want to see for myself that they're both okay and then we'll leave."

Unperturbed by her friend's outburst, Gemma replied, "Well, fine, but I have to tell you, I picked a hell of a time to quit smoking."

"You should have quit years ago," Kelly said distractedly,

looking out the car window at the sign that flashed by declaring, "Welcome to Briar Hollow."

Gemma sighed. "So you've been telling me since we were 16 years old."

They drove a couple of blocks in silence until, out of the corner of her eye, Gemma saw Kelly thumb on the screen of her smartphone -- yet again. "Anything from the girls?" she asked.

"No," Kelly said worriedly. "Nothing."

"You know," Gemma ventured, "they might have just gone somewhere for the evening."

Even though she hadn't wanted to talk about it, Kelly knew that Gemma knew *exactly* what was going on. Now Kelly had no choice but to say so and open the door on a discussion she didn't want to have. Taking a deep breath, she admitted quietly, "Something isn't right, Gemma. I can feel it . . . like I used to feel things."

The odd sensation had begun earlier that day. The unease rustled vaguely at the edge of her perception, growing in intensity with each passing hour. It hadn't been there in so many years, Kelly had forgotten the persistence of that inner voice demanding to be acknowledged.

"Can you get a read on what it's trying to tell you?" Gemma asked.

Kelly shook her head. "I don't remember how."

Keeping her eyes on the road, Gemma said, "Sure you do, honey. Come on. Open your mind. What are you feeling exactly?"

"I can't, Gemma," she said stubbornly, her voice taking on equal parts fear and anxiety.

"Yes, you can," Gemma replied just as obstinately. "You're right here with me and you're perfectly safe. What does it feel like?"

The smaller woman huddled in the passenger seat. She held

herself tightly, cautiously opening the tiniest possible channel in her mind.

"A gateway," she said finally.

Gemma frowned. "It feels like a gateway?" she asked. "You mean the gateway to Shevington?"

Kelly shook her head. "I don't think so," she said. "This is an opening that was never meant to be."

"What's that supposed to mean?"

"You know it doesn't work that like!" Kelly said, frustration filling her words. "I don't get a whole picture. That's the problem!"

"Okay, okay, calm down," Gemma said, pulling the car onto the town square. "We're here, so we'll get it all figured out soon enough."

She guided the vehicle down the alley and parked behind Jinx's red Prius. When the women got out, they both looked toward the upstairs windows. No lights burned inside, but the glow from a nearby guard lamp illuminated four pairs of feline eyes.

"That must be Tori's new apartment," Gemma said, indicating the addition on the back of the building. Those windows were dark as well.

Kelly dug in her enormous, over-sized handbag and produced a single key on a give-away ring from the First National Bank of Briar Hollow.

"Hopefully this will still work," she said.

"If it won't," Gemma said, rummaging in her own bag, "maybe this one will." She held up an identical key.

In the dim light, Kelly smiled. "You kept yours, too?" she asked.

"I did," Gemma nodded. "Never say never, Kell. Go on, try yours."

Kelly inserted the key in the lock, smiling slightly when the tumblers slid effortlessly into place.

When they were safely inside, Kelly closed the door and turned the deadbolt. The interior of the shop was completely quiet. Gemma took a small flashlight out of her purse and played the beam around the ground floor.

"Nothing looks out of place," she whispered.

"Myrtle isn't here," Kelly said, "is she?"

Gemma shook her head. "I don't think so," she said. "The place feels too . . . still."

Moving into the center of the building, they looked around the espresso bar and then peered into the storeroom.

"Let's go downstairs," Gemma suggested.

Kelly paled. "Do you really think we should?" she asked.

"Why not?" Gemma asked. "We've spent hours down there training with Myrtle."

"That was a long time ago," Kelly said tentatively.

"Yes," Gemma said, "but it might be the only way we can figure out where the girls are. I mean, honestly, Kell, they've probably gone to The Valley."

"We're *not* going there," the other woman replied instantly.

"I didn't say anything about us going there," Gemma soothed. "Let's just go down and have a look."

Reluctantly, Kelly followed her to the top of the stairs, but when Gemma turned on the light, they saw nothing but a gloomy, cluttered mess below.

"See," Kelly said, "we're not allowed into the first stage of the in between now."

Gemma turned toward her. "Are you honestly going to tell me you don't remember how to get around that?" she asked.

Taking a step backward, Kelly said, "We don't do magic any more."

"I think we've covered that already," Gemma replied.

"Then we need to cover it again because you're not listening to me," Kelly said, taking Gemma's arm and trying to pull her out of the doorway.

Gemma didn't budge. "Just because we don't do magic anymore," she said, "doesn't mean we don't still know *how* to do magic. You insisted we come over here because you felt one of your premonitions. Did you ever stop to think that might have bigger implications?"

Kelly frowned. "Like what?" she asked.

"Like Jinx coming into her powers might be reawakening your abilities," Gemma replied.

A look of horror washed over Kelly's face. "What do you mean reawaken? Why would you even say something like that?"

Gemma held out her hand and whispered, "*Orbis*."

A shimmering globe of light appeared over her palm, rose a few inches in the air, and began to rotate slowly.

Kelly regarded her now with open horror. "Oh my God, Gemma, put that out! Now!"

"No, honey," she said, "I won't. Come on. You try it."

"I don't want to try it," Kelly declared firmly. "I can't do that any more and I don't want to."

Gemma studied her friend's face in the half-light from the doorway. "Okay," she said finally, "if you stand right there and make an honest effort to access your magic and you can't do it, we'll close this door, sit down, and just wait for the girls to come back."

Although she looked doubtful about the wisdom of the whole experiment, Kelly raised her hand. The fingers trembled slightly, but she held her palm up just as Gemma had done and whispered, "*Orbis*."

Instantly a second globe of light appeared, rose to an equal level with Gemma's own ball of light, and began to rotate slowly in time with it.

"See," Gemma said triumphantly, "I told you."

Kelly's eyes widened as she watched the glowing spheres. "I can't believe it," she said finally.

Gemma whispered, "*Dissolvo*." Her light blinked out.

Kelly repeated the incantation, and the second light was instantly extinguished.

They stood silent for a heartbeat and then Kelly squared her shoulders.

"So," she said, "are we going down there or what?"

Gemma stepped aside and grinned. "After you," she said.

Kelly descended into the basement one halting step at a time with Gemma following behind. At the bottom of the stairs, they turned toward each other. Gemma held out her hands. "Ready?" she asked.

"Yes," Kelly said, interlocking their fingers.

Awkwardly at first and then with growing confidence, the two women began to recite in Gaelic. Slowly the room filled with light and the dim outline of objects coalesced, overlaying and then supplanting the visible scene. As they spoke the final words of the spell, rows of shelves solidified before them, and the area by the fireplace settled into focus. They both opened their eyes at the same time, still holding hands.

Kelly looked around and whispered, awestruck, "Oh my God, Gem, we did it."

Before Gemma could answer, a voice from under the stairs said, "So you did, and I cannot tell you how much I appreciate you saving me the trouble of finding a way to dismantle the aos sí's defenses."

Without thinking, Gemma stepped slightly in front of Kelly as a red-haired woman emerged from the gloom.

"Who are you?" Gemma demanded. "How did you get in here?"

"My name is Brenna Sinclair," the woman said. "And I got in here because you let me in."

Gemma paled, but she stood her ground. "You're the witch Knasgowa bound to her grave."

Brenna inclined her head to one side and studied Gemma. "Very good," she said. "Let me guess, you are Tori's mother."

"I am," Gemma said.

"You are of my blood," Brenna said, studying her appraisingly. "Why do you defy me, daughter?"

"I am not your daughter," Gemma spat out. "I stand with the daughters of Knasgowa, like my mother and her mother before me."

"Hmm," Brenna said approvingly, "you have fire. I like that. The quality has potential. But that trembling little bird hiding in your shadow? Can this actually be Jinx's mother?"

"You stay away from her," Gemma said angrily.

"Step out so I can see you, little bird," Brenna cooed. "Or are you too afraid?"

At the taunting, Kelly raised her chin. "I'm not afraid of you," she said, moving to stand beside Gemma.

"Oh, but you should be," Brenna replied, "you should be very afraid, or the consequences of your bravery may be quite tragic . . . for your daughters."

Kelly bristled. "You leave our daughters out of this," she snapped.

Brenna laughed. "Ah, the mother mouse who roared," she said. "I'm afraid I cannot leave your daughters out of this. After all, Jinx is the one who set me free."

When Kelly's face paled, she said, "Ah, perhaps Jinx did not tell you about the events of this summer in proper detail. Yes, your darling daughter is now reaping what she has sown."

Gemma regarded her coldly. "Get to the point," she said. "What do you want?"

"What do I want?" Brenna repeated, her lips curling in a sardonic smile. "Why, I want you to take me to the entrance to Shevington, of course."

"And if we don't?" Gemma asked.

"Well then, my dear, " Brenna answered, "I'm afraid you'll have far worse on your conscience than two dead cheerleaders."

22

As I expected, Tori was still awake when I went up to our rooms after my evening with Chase. We stayed up into the wee hours talking about everything that had happened since we'd left the store. Our bodies were running on Shevington time, so it had been a long, full day. Still, Tori couldn't stop talking about going to the stables with Moira and Amity to feed apples to Blissia and the other unicorns, and I couldn't stop telling the story about the game of Red Dot. Well, first I couldn't stop talking about Chase saying he loved me, and *then* I couldn't stop talking about Red Dot.

Ultimately silly exhaustion took over. Anyone listening would have thought we were the ones who had been playing a drinking game. Every time I recounted Festus' epic face plant on the pool table felt, we fell into renewed fits of giggling. I think we literally laughed ourselves to sleep. I have no idea what time that happened, but when the morning sun rising over the Mother Tree awakened me, I was curled up on the couch and Tori had all but disappeared into the mountain of pillows piled up on the window seat.

"Hey," I whispered, "I have to meet Chase to go watch the

Brown Mountain guard drill. Don't forget we're supposed to be at Aunt Fiona's at 9 o'clock for breakfast."

Tori mumbled something like, "Amity won't let me forget," before rolling over and falling right back to sleep.

Chase was waiting for me in the lobby. "Good morning," I said, accepting a kiss. "How's your father today?"

"Cranky," Chase laughed.

"He's always cranky," I pointed out.

"Okay, cranky-er," Chase said. "Last I saw him he was holding an ice pack on his head with one paw and dipping the other in his coffee."

It was my turn to laugh. "Why wasn't he just drinking the coffee?" I asked.

"He said his tongue is too loud," Chase snickered. "Serves him right."

We stepped out on the square into glorious morning light. "Speaking of coffee," I said. "Any chance I can get a cup before we go watch the aerial drills?"

"Absolutely," Chase said. "Follow me."

He led me to a small shop on the corner where we bought steaming mugs of coffee and buttery croissants. We ate as we strolled toward the fairy barracks. Chase pointed out businesses and introduced me to people on the street. After several blocks, I noticed my drink was exactly the same temperature as it had been when I accepted the cup from Chase.

"Man," I said, "I'd like to get cups with insulation like this for our coffee shop."

"They're not insulated," Chase said, "they're enchanted, but I can get the lady who runs the shop to teach you the spell if you like."

"Very funny," I replied. "I don't think Myrtle would be too happy if we started handing out magical coffee mugs."

"She might if they said 'Made at Myrtle's,'" he suggested helpfully.

I almost spit my coffee laughing, which only put a broader grin on his face.

"How long have you known Myrtle?" I asked.

"All my life," he answered. "The librarian look is new, but it kind of suits her. She can get awfully cranky when she thinks you're not catching on to something fast enough, but the heart of the aos sí is filled with love."

"Do you have any idea how old she really is?"

"No," he said, "but she is certainly one of the oldest Fae on the earth."

"And Moira?" I asked.

"She and Barnaby came to the New World together," Chase answered.

"Together as in *together*?" I asked.

"No one has ever really been sure about that," Chase said. "Barnaby had a wife, but she was killed by the Creavit."

"And Moira?"

"She has worked as a sole practitioner for centuries," he said, "but there is no one to whom she is closer than Barnaby, not even Myrtle."

We rounded a corner and suddenly I was looking at an open field swarming with fairies in battle fatigues. As we watched, a squadron of 24 launched skyward and broken into three groups.

"Those are called 'flights'," Chase explained as we climbed onto a viewing stand at the end of the field. "They'll do some close formation drills and then stage dogfights."

"At which my lads excel!" a voice boomed right beside my ear.

I jumped straight up, but miraculously, my coffee didn't spill. That's when I realized the cup wasn't emptying out. Perma-hot, self-filling, and spill proof? Now *that* was my idea of a coffee cup.

Ironweed suddenly appeared in front of my face, beret in hand. "I'm sorry, Beautiful," he said. "I didn't mean to scare you like that." Turning to Chase he grinned and said, "Well, would you look at what the cat dragged in!"

"You should see dad," Chase countered.

"I heard," Ironweed said, hovering out of the way as I sat back down. "It's all over town you took him out of The Dirty Claw by the scruff of his neck."

"I did *not* scruff him," Chase said. "That would just be disrespectful . . . and besides, he passed out before I had to."

We all laughed at that.

Ironweed said, "May I?" before neatly landing on Chase's shoulder.

Chase glanced down at him and said, "Are your boots clean?"

"You are such a neat freak, McGregor," Ironweed replied. "And yes, they're clean. Hello? Fairy? Flying?"

For the next half-hour the diminutive major explained the guard's training regimen to me. "It's mostly evasive tactics," he said, chewing on a miniscule cigar. "Can't have one of the lads getting captured by the humans. But if we need to, we can swarm. It's a matter of creating mass confusion. Been my experience that humans aren't good with big bugs. That's what they tell themselves we are. Of course, with the rise of the insecticide industry we've had to make gas masks standard issue gear. Getting hit with a blast of that stuff right in the kisser is no fun."

He sounded like a combat veteran discussing chemical warfare, which I guess, he is, now that I think about it.

"Why exactly are you engaging with humans?" I asked.

"We try not to," Ironweed said, "but there's more than one way into The Valley. Won't do to have some random camper see anyone come walking out of thin air. The drills over at Brown Mountain are to keep most of the sightseeing investigator types over in that direction. As for the immediate area around Briar Hollow, we conduct reconnaissance flights to map the location of hikers and campers at all times. We temporarily close portals in areas where there's any chance of one of ours being seen."

"You sound like an air traffic controller," I observed.

His whole face lit up. "Have you ridden on one of the big planes?" he asked.

"Sure, lots of times."

"What I wouldn't give to fly that high," he said wistfully. "Oxygen deprivation and cold kicks us in the tail feathers."

"Couldn't you just sneak onto a flight?" I asked.

He looked at me like I was crazy. "With all the security after 9/11? Not a chance," he said.

I couldn't resist. "Ironweed," I said, "people get stuff past the TSA all the time. Are you telling me a fairy couldn't make it on an airplane?"

"I'm telling you we wouldn't try," he replied stoutly.

"Why not?"

"Because we're *American* fairies," he declared. "We're not going to do anything to complicate security for our human brothers in arms."

For just an instant, I felt like I was in a scene from *Honey, Rambo Shrunk the Kids*, but Ironweed was completely sincere. Lesson learned. Patriotism comes in all shapes and sizes.

A little before 9 o'clock, we excused ourselves and walked to Aunt Fiona's cottage, which sat at the bottom of the hill on the east end of town just inside the city wall. The thatched house looked like something out of a storybook with its white picket fence and riotous garden.

Chase led me around to the side gate, which he held open. We found my aunt, Tori, and Amity in rapt conversation with an 8-foot-tall shaggy Chewbacca sort wearing galoshes and a tweed suit.

"Bigfoot is wearing clothes?" I whispered to Chase under my breath as we approached.

"Barnaby's rule," Chase said. "He's a bit straight-laced."

"Did anybody stop to think Sasquatch might need a little fashion help?" I asked, snickering.

Trying to keep a straight face, Chase, said, "Stan! How are you big guy! This is Fiona's niece, Jinx."

The faint odor of wet dog hosed down with men's cologne wafted past my nose. Then my hand disappeared into a massive paw and Stan's deep voice rumbled through my chest.

"I'm so pleased to finally meet you," he said. "Fiona talks about you all the time! I knew you'd be pretty, but wow! She said you have cats. I just love cats."

Without thinking, I blurted out, "*You* love cats?"

Stan's hearty guffaw echoed through the garden. "Sasquatch are vegetarians, Jinx," he said. "And pacifists. Don't believe what you see in the movies. I raise bunnies, too."

Bigfoot raises bunny rabbits.

There may be hope for this world yet.

Blushing, I said, "I'm sorry, Stan, that was rude of me."

"Naw," he said, "I take some getting used to. It's okay."

"Stanley is an expert gardener," Aunt Fiona said, pouring a cup of tea for me. "His roses have taken the Shevington cup for five years running."

"What's your secret?" I asked, mainly just to be polite. I was in no way prepared for his answer.

"Unicorn manure," he replied placidly.

This time I managed not to choke on the hot liquid I was swallowing. "Really," I said, trying to sound studious, "isn't that supposed to be rainbow colored?"

"Depends on what you feed them," he said, without missing a beat. "I prefer the blue manure. The rainbow stuff is a little too acidic for roses."

"Stanley," Amity said, "I am so glad you said that. I was having a conversation with that insufferable Hester McElroy about wolf's bane . . .

Before she could finish speaking, a shadow passed over the table where we were seated, followed in rapid succession by five others. We all looked up to find my dragonlet friends circling the garden.

"Oh for heaven's sake," Fiona said with annoyance. "They know they're not supposed to be flying over the city. Stanley, have you been feeding them again."

"No, Fiona," he said, holding up one shaggy paw. "Scout's honor."

"Uh, I think they're looking for me," I said. "I made friends with them down in the meadow before we got to the city."

Fiona's eyes widened. "You made *friends* with dragonlets?" she asked, clearly shocked. "My dear, that simply isn't done."

"Sorry," I shrugged. "I didn't get the memo."

Just then Tori cried, "Look out! Incoming!"

Reacting to the warning, I put out my hand and neatly caught a gold pocket watch and chain as they plummeted toward the table. When I realized what I was holding, my blood turned to ice. I clicked open the case just to be certain and sure enough, there was the inscription Beau had shown me when he first told me the story about James McGregor finding his body on the battlefield. The words read, "To Brother Beauregard T. Longworth, Master Mason, with gratitude for his service. Harmony Lodge No. 1."

When I looked up, Tori was watching me closely. "Is that what I think it is?" she asked.

"Yes," I said. "It's Beau's pocket watch. I don't know what's going on, but we've got to get home. Now."

23

We threw our belongings into our packs and rushed out of the Inn. Chase, Festus, Myrtle, and Darby met us downstairs with their packs slung over their shoulders. Chase had apparently filled Festus in about the pocket watch. The old cat seemed fully and miraculously recovered from his hangover. He was riding in the mesh compartment, but with his head sticking out through the partially open cover so he could take in the sights.

"Barnaby and Moira will join us at the city gate," Myrtle said, as we all started across the lawn under the Mother Tree.

I didn't have the presence of mind to ask why. The sense of alarm I'd felt when I looked at Beau's pocket watch in my hand was getting stronger, and for some reason I couldn't get my mother's face out of my mind. So when Myrtle spoke to me, I just nodded and kept plowing forward. The straps of my backpack were cutting into my arms and without thinking -- or warning Rodney -- I shifted to find a better position.

The rat let out a protesting yelp, and a voice from the vicinity of my knee said, "Rodney may ride with me, Mistress, if it would be easier."

When I looked down, I saw Darby's concerned face looking up at me. "Thank you, Darby," I said, stopping long enough to make my arm a stable pathway for the Rodney who gratefully abandoned my shoulder and ran down to the waiting brownie.

"Sorry, Rodney," I added as I watched him settle himself on Darby's pack and clip himself in with his safety strap.

That won me a reproachful rodent glare, but there was nothing I could do to make peace with him at the moment. Later there would be junk food and fulsome apologies, then, I just settled my pack more comfortably on my shoulders.

I did, however, think to ask Darby about his absence over the past few hours. "Have you been with Dewey all this time?" I said.

"Yes, Mistress," Darby said, sounding chagrined. "I am so sorry. Did you have need of me?"

"Don't apologize, Darby," I said. "I'm just glad you had a good time . . ."

The words came out of my mouth just as we passed under the first shading branches of the Mother Tree. This time I stopped because she told me to, in a loud, clear voice that echoed through my mind drowning out all other sights and sounds.

"At the gateway you will face a choice," the Tree said. "Remember, child, that which appears weakest may in truth be your greatest strength. Now, go and face your destiny."

Destiny.

Not a great word at plot points like that one.

The word "destiny" is about as ominous as that moment in a horror flick when one of the campers goes into the woods alone. I always feel like yelling at the screen, "You know you're going to get killed, right?"

"Destiny" was not penciled in on my morning schedule, but at least according to the Mother Tree, we had an appointment anyway.

It would have been appropriate for dramatic music to swell in the background, but as the Tree's voice faded in my mind, the bustling sounds of Shevington came back to full volume around me. Myrtle looked at me with understanding. "The Mother Tree spoke to you," she said, but the words weren't a question.

"Did you hear what she said?" I asked.

Myrtle shook her head. "The Tree speaks in confidence," she replied, "but heed well her words."

Uh, yeah, except I had no idea what the words *meant*.

At the gate, our group didn't even slow down. Barnaby and Moira simply fell in step with us. Trust me, when you walk in Shevington beside the Lord High Mayor nobody asks if you're supposed to be there. Bill Ruff was still guarding his little bridge, but this time he doffed his cap and wished us a good morning, even adding, "Well met, aos sí," as we passed.

I heard Myrtle mutter, "That's more like it, you old goat," which elicited a low rumble from Bill. From what I can tell, they each enjoy tormenting the other.

We crossed the meadow in half the time we'd taken with our leisurely stroll the day before. I hadn't noticed then that a small cairn of stones marks the gateway, which is where we halted. Barnaby turned toward me, "Moira and I have come with you because we believe that Brenna Sinclair may be on the other side of this portal."

Now they were telling me?

"How do you know that?" I asked. "And if she is in the basement, why are we just standing here?"

Moira answered. "The place you call the basement is the Shevington archive," she said. "It exists in another layer of the in between, one that is heavily warded. Both Myrtle and I experienced a disturbance in the energy of the wards at the same moment this morning. We are standing here, as you say, because we must proceed carefully."

Beside me, Tori said, "Use the Force, Luke," under her breath.

The wisecracks tend to go up a notch when she's nervous, but the thing is, she wasn't really wrong. Now I understand that Myrtle and Moira really do sense changes in the energy field that is all life, and they were completely right about being careful. The thing is? Destiny took "careful" off the plate.

IN THE BASEMENT

BEAU LONGWORTH AND JAMES MCGREGOR heard voices approaching. Without having to confer, they both faded to near invisibility and retreated deeper into the stacks. As they watched, Kelly and Gemma approached the door to Shevington, walking in front of Brenna Sinclair.

"We won't do it," Gemma said angrily.

"Oh, but you will," Brenna replied complacently. "Because if you don't, I won't kill you. I'll make sure you live long lives with vivid memories of your daughters' deaths playing out in your mind every single moment. You only heard about that unfortunate car accident in your girlhood. You didn't see it."

Although her face had gone deathly white, Kelly's voice was surprisingly strong. "I saw," she said. "I went down to the Ford motor company and looked at the car when the wrecker towed it down from the mountains. I saw the blood all over the seats. Their pom poms were soaked with it."

Brenna chuckled. "What a deliciously vivid image," she said without a trace of compassion. "Now, imagine your darling daughter's body soaked with her own blood. I am quite skilled at the art of protracting death."

"Even if we get you through the opening," Gemma said,

"what makes you think Moira will perform *Veneficus Trajectio* for you?"

"For the same reason the two of you have so compliantly joined me here," Brenna said. "You are infected with the weakest of all diseases: love. You abandoned your high-minded defiance the instant I threatened your puny spawn, and Moira will do the same when I kill Barnaby Shevington and begin to lay waste to their precious sanctuary. She will bow to one to protect the many."

"What makes you think you can fight Barnaby and win?" Kelly asked in a tight voice.

"Because he is a man of principle," Brenna said. "I killed his wife and he sought no retribution. Instead he gathered up his little flock of sheep and fled to a new land. Barnaby Shevington will not stand in my way. Before the sun sets this day in The Valley, I will have my full powers again. Now, open the portal."

"No," Gemma said stubbornly. "If you're such a high and mighty sorceress, do it yourself."

The two women now stood with their backs to the door facing Brenna, who feigned an aggrieved expression. "Very well," she said. "I did not want it to come to this."

She extended one long finger in Kelly's direction. The smaller woman let out a surprised gasp, her hands going to her neck. Then she fell to her knees, looking wildly at Gemma. "I . . . can't breathe," she wheezed. "She's choking me."

Gemma's head swiveled between Kelly and Brenna. "Let her go," she snapped. "If you're such a big bad witch, pick on someone your own size."

Brenna crooked her finger and Kelly fell forward, catching herself with her hands. Strangled, drowning noises emanated from her throat.

"Now where would the fun be in that?" Brenna asked. "Are

your convictions strong enough to allow you to stand here and watch your best friend die?"

Kelly managed to wheeze, "Don't do it, Gem."

That entreaty, not Brenna's threats, broke Gemma's resolve.

"Let her go," she said. "I'll do it."

With a wave of her hand, Brenna released Kelly.

Gemma helped her friend stand. With her hands still on Kelly's arms, she said, "I'm sorry, honey, but we have to do it together, like we did in the old days."

A flicker of recognition moved through Kelly's eyes. "It's okay," she said. "I'm ready."

Brenna made an impatient sound in the back of her throat. "Please," she said, "I have no desire to play witness to your sentimentality. Get on with it."

"No problem," Gemma said, "but you're getting ready to bite off more than you can chew, lady."

In the meadow

"I'm sorry," I said, "but could we get a move on here. If Brenna is on the other side, let's just do this thing and get it over with."

Moira and Myrtle exchanged a look I didn't like, but they could explain all the metaphysical mumbo jumbo to me later. My Spidey sense was literally screaming. Whatever was happening on the other side of that door was *not* good. Every fiber of my being told me we had to get home and take care of business. *Now.*

"Very well," Moira said, "but I suggest you all stand back."

She raised her hand and began to chant the words Myrtle had used to open the door, but nothing happened. Barnaby moved to stand beside her. They recited the spell in unison, and

I saw the air above the cairn of rocks ripple, but the door refused to open.

"*So* not good," Tori said.

"Ya think?" I asked.

Darby was standing between us, with Rodney on his shoulders. Chase was on my left. I heard the sound of a zipper being pulled and looked over to see Festus open his compartment farther so he could stand up taller and put his forepaws on his son's shoulder.

Myrtle joined the magical firing line and the trio began the spell again. This time the portal did open, to reveal a full-blown firefight on the other side -- between our mothers and Brenna Sinclair.

I'd like to give you the full blow by blow of what happened next, but it was literally all a blur. Before I knew what was happening, Festus was over Chase's shoulder. In mid-air the old yellow tomcat transformed into a mountain lion. I caught a glimpse of a gray muzzle, a mass of gnarled scar tissue covering one hip, and a surprising amount of rippling muscle. The force of the leap sent Chase sprawling backward. As he went down, he slammed into me and we both wound up in a heap on the ground.

Somehow Rodney was loose, and tearing through the opening after Festus with Darby in hot pursuit. The portal let out a static burst of bright orange light, and slammed shut.

The Mother Tree's words rose in my mind. "That which appears weakest may in truth be your greatest strength."

I hoped she was right, because at that very moment, a three-legged mountain lion, a rat, a brownie, and our mothers were doing battle with Brenna Sinclair.

As I struggled to stand up, a sob tore at my throat. I felt Chase's arms go around me and I buried my head in his shoulder. A hand touched my back, and I knew it was Tori.

If Festus, Rodney, Darby, and the moms died, their deaths would be on me. I was the one who had foolishly set Brenna free. I was the one who arrogantly tried to use my powers with no understanding of the possible consequences. Black despair slammed down around me.

Under my ear, Chase's voice rumbled. "Get that damn door open," he growled. "We have to get in there."

"We can't," Myrtle said.

"What do you mean you can't!" he said. "You're the aos sí. You control the fairy mound."

I didn't have to see Myrtle's face to understand the gravity of her words. "My dear boy," she said softly, "no one controls the fairy mound."

24

Kelly and Gemma clasped hands and held each other's gaze. Together they began to speak, keeping their voices so low, Brenna had to strain to hear what they were saying. By the time she realized what the two women were doing, it was too late.

"Stop!" she roared, moving toward them only to be repelled by the protective barrier they were building around themselves. Kelly's eyes began to glow a soft blue first and then the aquamarine fire bled into Gemma's gaze. At that moment, they turned, dropping the barrier and hurling bolts of energy at Brenna, who screeched and threw up her hands, deflecting the fire at the last possible moment.

The wall behind them rippled, but neither Kelly nor Gemma realized the portal had opened until a massive, tawny mountain lion landed beside Kelly.

"Need a little help, darling?" the big cat asked, glaring at Brenna and drawing back his lips in a snarling hiss that revealed razor-sharp fangs.

"Festus?" Kelly said, not taking her attention away from the sorceress. "Is that you?"

"Of course, it's me," the cat said, drawing himself up. "Let's take this bitch down."

Festus launched himself at Brenna, striking her in the chest and driving her to the floor. Gathering her will, Brenna hit him with a blast of energy, but the amulet gave her only a fraction of her former strength. Even with only three good legs, Festus righted himself in mid-air and landed on his feet.

"That all you've got?" he taunted, circling her slowly, his long tail wagging lazily behind him. "This is gonna be fun."

Brenna strained to divide her limited powers between the werecats and the two witches, who were now chanting at a different and more confident cadence. Glancing down, she realized that dark green fibrous tendrils had begun to grow around her feet, weaving themselves tighter and tighter into a dense net.

Panicked gripped her. Where was her focus? How best to channel her few resources? "Stop!" she ordered Festus. "Stand still!"

"What's the matter?" Festus purred, still pacing around her. "Can't keep up?"

Catching her foot against the rising green webbing, Brenna stumbled. Before she could right herself, her blouse fell open and the amber amulet spilled out.

"The necklace!" Darby cried. "The amulet! Take if off her neck!"

Out of nowhere, Rodney joined the fight. The instant he'd come through the portal, the rat sought safety in the shadows, climbing to a high perch on one of the shelves. Now, he was in perfect position to launch himself at the trapped sorceress, tangling himself in her thick mane of red hair and sending her into a frenzy of panicked revulsion.

"Get off of me you filthy rat!" she screamed, flailing wildly at her own head.

Deftly dodging the assault, Rodney dropped onto her

shoulder and began searching around her neck for the clasp to the chain. When she felt him touch her skin, Brenna's cries intensified.

Festus seized the opportunity to lunge at the frantic woman, raking his claws down her arm. Blood immediately soaked the torn fabric. The maneuver bought Rodney the time he needed, but pausing to unfasten the clasp made him vulnerable. At just the same instant the necklace broke free; Brenna hit the rat with a direct body blow that sent him flying in one direction and the amulet in another -- straight into Beau Longworth's hand.

The instant the Colonel's fingers closed over the stone, his form solidified. Color flowed down his body, turning the braid on his tunic a glistening gold and blacking the scarred leather of his boots. Sensing rather than understanding the transformation, determination filled eyes that were once again the color of the sea. Drawing his cavalry saber and stepping forward, Beau plunged the blade directly in Brenna Sinclair's heart.

Everyone froze in place. Utter silence filled the room. Brenna looked down at her chest, then back up at Beau with an expression of stunned astonishment. Blood bubbled at her lips, spilling down onto her chest, and falling onto the green net that had now climbed as high as her waist. The instant the blood touched the tendrils, flames engulfed Brenna and in an instant, she was gone.

Beau stood rooted in place, the amulet in one hand and his sword, the blade now completely clean, firmly in the other. James McGregor, pale and ghostly, stepped out of the stacks.

"Brother Longworth," he said, his voice filled with awe, "you are alive."

Looking down at his own body, Beau shook his head. "That cannot be," he said simply.

A sound beside him made Beau look down. Darby was

standing next to him. "Excuse me, sir," the brownie said. "But you are not really alive."

"If you know what has happened to me, Master Darby," Beau said. "I would be most grateful for an explanation."

"You are holding the Amulet of the Phoenix," Darby said.

Beau looked down at the necklace in his hand. "The bird that rose anew from the flames," he said softly.

"Yes, sir," Darby said. "So long as you have it in your possession, you may walk among the living, but it cannot raise you from the dead."

Gemma joined them. "It did a good enough job in my book," she said, holding her hand out to Beau. "I'm Tori's mother."

Remembering himself, Beau hastily put away his sword, and swept off his hat. Bowing low, he kissed Gemma's hand. Then he turned to Kelly, "And you are Miss Jinx's mother?" he asked.

"Yes," Kelly said. She looked shaken, but there was also a gleam of triumph in her red-rimmed eyes.

Beau bowed again. "I am deeply honored to have been of service to you, Madame. I love your daughter as if she were my own girl. You must be enormously proud of her."

Tears spilled out of Kelly's eyes and rolled down her cheeks. "I am," she said, "and I hope she's going to be proud of me now."

"I think, Madame, that she will be proud of us all," Beau said.

A sound made them turn toward the stacks as Festus came limping out of the shadows holding Rodney gently in his mouth.

"Rodney!" Darby cried, rushing forward.

"Easy there," Festus ordered out of the corner of his mouth. "He's not dead. Just got a busted leg."

Darby gently took Rodney from Festus and cradled the rat against his chest. "You were so brave, Rodney," he crooned softly. "I cannot wait to tell the story, and I will take very good care of you until you are well again."

Rodney weakly held up one front paw and gave them all the thumbs up sign.

Behind them, the portal burst open with a flash of light. Chase, in his mountain lion form, landed in a menacing crouch. Jinx and Tori rushed through the opening, followed by Barnaby, Moira, and Myrtle. Then they all stopped and blinked in confusion at the scene before them.

"Well," Festus said, sitting down with studied disdain and regarding their would-be rescuers, "about time you slackers showed up."

"Dad!" Chase cried. "Are you okay? What happened?"

"Of course, I'm okay, boy," Festus answered crossly. "I was getting in fights with wizards before you were even weaned. We killed Brenna Sinclair, that's what happened. What did you think we were going to do? Invite the woman to tea?"

Clearly dumbfounded, Jinx looked at her mother. "You killed Brenna?" she asked numbly.

Blushing and embracing her daughter, Kelly said, self-deprecatingly, "Well, not me specifically, dear. We all did."

Tori gave her own mother a big hug and then, holding Gemma at arm's length said, "I think you have some explaining to do. I thought you said you two weren't very powerful."

"Well," Gemma hedged, "we might have downplayed that a little bit."

"Ya think?" Tori asked.

Then she spotted Darby holding Rodney. "Oh my God!" she cried. "Is Rodney okay?"

Darby nodded, but his lower lip quivered. "Yes, Mistress, but his leg is broken. Please help him."

"I will tend to him," Moira said, stepping forward. She led Darby over to a small table nearby and began to examine the injured rat with the worried brownie hovering at her elbow.

Kelly smiled at Jinx. "Don't you want to say hello to your friend?" she asked, nodding toward Beau.

Beau, still holding his hat in his hands, smiled shyly. "Hello, Miss Jinx," he said. The poor man barely had time to prepare himself before Jinx threw her arms around him. He folded her readily in his arms, but couldn't manage more than an embarrassed, "Oh my. There, there now."

"You're alive," Jinx sobbed. "You're all alive."

"Well, my dear," Beau said, "Master Darby tells me I'm not quite *alive* per se, but I am a good bit more functional than when last you saw me."

Myrtle cleared her throat. "Perhaps we should all adjourn to more comfortable surroundings and discuss what has occurred?" she suggested. "I think we may all have a great many questions."

"Capital idea," Barnaby said. "James? Will you join us?"

"My pleasure," the ghost said. "I haven't had this much entertainment in at least a century."

Jinx stepped away from Beau, but kept one arm around his waist. She held the other arm out to her mother, who moved beside her. Arm-in-arm, the three of them led the way toward the lair, with the others following behind. Chase and Festus brought up the rear.

As they padded along, Chase said, "Pretty impressive, old man."

"I'm not dead yet, boy," Festus said, "and don't you be forgetting it."

25

Myrtle was doing that understatement thing again when she said we all had a "great many" questions. By the time the moms and Beau explained their role in what happened that night, we had a fairly good picture of how it all came together. And then there was the big old hole right there in the basement wall.

Moira and Myrtle took care of that immediately, reforming the solid earth and taking possession of the miner's hat and lamp that Beau assured us had created the tunnel.

"I wish I knew who that old man was," I said, "and how he got in the store."

Festus, now restored to his usual housecat self, stretched languidly on the hearth and said, "I'll tell you exactly who that was. Fish Pike. His Dad was a werecat halfling. Couldn't make the change. It turned him into a bitter drunk. Fish has been chasing for a way to get up in The Valley since he was a boy. Don't you worry about him. Chase and I will pay a social call and make sure he doesn't ever do anything like that again."

"You're not going to hurt him, are you?" I asked.

"No," Chase said. He'd gone to his apartment just long

enough to change into human form and get fresh clothes and was now nursing a glass of Scotch in one of the chairs by the fire. "We won't hurt him, we'll just have a purposeful talk with him."

"Wait a minute," Tori said. "I thought you told us werecats always date their own kind."

"We do," Festus said. "You don't get the same kind of consequences if a werecat takes up with a human over another Fae, but if the offspring can't change, there's an envy that eats away at them and drives them crazy. It's like they're always trying to be something they're not, and their minds can't take it."

For as angry as I might have been at this Fish Pike person, what Festus described made me feel sorry for the old man. And it made me appreciate even more why the cantankerous old cat was concerned about my getting involved with his son.

In those few moments when the portal was closed and I couldn't get through to help the people I loved, the real message of that summer was driven home to me. Magic is an incredible responsibility. It is not to be ignored or taken lightly. Myrtle wanted a dedicated student? She got one that night.

During the whole exchange about Fish Pike, Moira had been sitting quietly, turning the filthy old cap over in her hands with a contemplative expression on her face.

At the first lull in the conversation, Barnaby asked her, "What are you thinking?"

Moira looked up, bringing her attention back to the group. The way her eyes met Barnaby's, I completely understood why no one was quite sure about those two.

"I am thinking that we are suddenly dealing with a rather large number of magical artifacts," Moira said. "And that there is no coincidence to that fact."

Barnaby nodded. "Irenaeus Chesterfield?" he asked.

"I believe so," she said. "Barnaby, I fear our better impulses where that man is concerned may have blinded us to his real activities. Irenaeus could, indeed, be an antiques dealer, but one with, I suspect, a quite specific specialty."

Beau cleared his throat. "And I surmise that this amulet is one of those objects," he said, holding it out to Moira. "I am quite prepared to give it over to you for safekeeping."

"Oh no, you're not!" I said stoutly. "You are putting that around your neck and wearing it."

The Colonel smiled at me. "It does not make me truly one of the living, Miss Jinx," he said. "A wise man does not go against the natural order of things."

"Nor does a wise man turn his back when fortune smiles on him," Barnaby said. "Please, Colonel Longworth, keep the amulet. Should we require its return, I am not concerned that you will refuse to comply."

Beau regarded the amulet, studying it carefully, and then he slowly fastened it around his neck and dropped the stone inside his shirt. "Thank you," he said simply. "I will not squander this gift."

Darby appeared out of nowhere and circulated among us with a silver platter of sandwiches. He sat a tray down in front of Rodney bearing a rather startling selection of cheeses. Technically, his leg was no longer broken thanks to Moira's healing magic, but Rodney had insisted on a cast anyway. He was installed on a little velvet pillow with one hind leg propped up accepting everyone's solicitous attention. We'd decided to indulge him and let him wear the cast for a week or so. After all, he had launched himself right at an evil sorceress without hesitation. If he wanted to be a drama rat now, he was entitled.

James McGregor was getting his own fair share of attention as well. In Myrtle's presence, he was solid enough to move objects and interact with his environment. He spent most of the evening studying the books in the shelves and listening to the rest of us talk. When Barnaby stood, looked at his own watch, and announced that he must be getting back, Beau invited James to take a walk with him.

"Uh, Beau," Tori said. "You can't go out like that."

The Colonel blinked at her. "Why not?" he asked.

"You're wearing a Civil War uniform," she said. "And a Confederate one at that."

Beau still didn't get it.

"It's 2015," Tori continued. "Come on, we need to get online and get you some new clothes. They can be here tomorrow at the latest."

James trailed along when they went upstairs, and then I walked the moms to the back door. Gemma left my Mom and me alone for a minute to exchange a private good-bye.

"Wow, Mom," I said. "That's pretty much all I've got. I don't know what to say."

She gave me a delighted smile. "I guess I did alright, didn't I?"

"From what I can tell, you were amazing," I said. "I'm so proud of you."

Mom looked down, a little uncertain. "Myrtle thinks we should start our training again, me and Gemma," she said haltingly. "How would you feel about that?"

"I think it's a fantastic idea," I said, and I meant it. "I'll get to spend more time with you."

The look of pure joy she gave me was worth everything we'd been through that night. As I watched her go down the back steps and join Gemma in the car, there was a spring in her step I'd never seen before, and I liked it.

Before I headed back downstairs, I heard Beau's scandalized voice inside Tori's apartment. "A gentleman does not go out by day without his coat, Miss Tori. It simply isn't done."

Laughing a little, I went back downstairs only to discover that Amity had gone home, and Myrtle was walking Moira and

Barnaby back to the portal. Festus was snoring on the hearth, and Chase was staring into the flames. "Want one?" he asked, holding up his glass.

"Please," I said, sitting down. "Neat."

Chase raised his eyebrows, but he didn't say anything when he poured me a couple of fingers of single malt and refilled his own glass. When we were both settled by the fire, he said, "How are you handling all of this?"

"Amazingly well," I said, "and mentioning amazing . . . "

"What?" he asked.

"You," I answered, "as a mountain lion. Tonight was the first time I've seen you change."

He regarded me silently. "And?" he finally asked.

"You are one studly hunk of kitty cat," I said, giving him a wicked grin.

Although I saw him blush a little, Chase laughed. "Thank you," he said, inclining his glass toward me.

Neither one of us said anything, and after a bit, Chase's own soft snores joined the louder ones emanating from his father. Careful not to wake him, I took the glass out of his hand and draped a blanket over his knees. Then I just sat down and looked at him.

Chase was, indeed, a magnificent mountain lion -- with large teeth and sharp talons that could, no doubt, inflict fatal injuries. Had he ever killed anyone? Could he kill someone if circumstances warranted it? What were the real implications of being with a man who carried such a completely different soul nestled deep in his being? Those were complex questions, none of which I would answer that night, but I wasn't running from them, and for the time being, that was enough.

EPILOGUE

The little witch could hear the rise and fall of voices from the apartment behind the store, but the girl, Tori, the one who ran the coffee bar, and the two men were completely absorbed in their online shopping. God, how she missed shopping, and the Internet, and texting, and being more than three-inches tall! She couldn't even think about the state of her complexion without bursting into tears.

Putting aside those thoughts, which only made her situation more unbearable, the witch stepped off the cup and inflated herself. What a night. She had seen it all, and it was better than a pay-per-view movie, but with her limited ability to send dispatches to her master, there was only so much she could tell him. It didn't matter anyway, though. He just wanted to know the ending. He wouldn't care about the brave rat or the sword play or the happy reunion.

A pang of guilt shot through her. These seemed like such decent people. Not the kind who would shrink a person, turn their skin green, and plaster them on a cup just for wanting a lock of Elvis' hair so much they were willing to steal it. They would understand how Elvis had been the only thing that had seen her through the trouble-twisted story that had been her life before.

Sighing, she pushed off the shelf on her broom and flew to the chessboard, laboriously moving the pieces to arrange the latest message. Thank God she'd learn to read music so she could be in the high school marching band. It wasn't as good as being a twirler, even though she'd tried to make the squad every year, but some dreams just aren't meant to be.

When all the pieces were in place, the witch tapped the corner of the board to activate the transmission and then flew back to her shelf. She heard the pawns signaling their position, and even though the sound was flat, she had the sequence right. In fact, the lyric was now stuck in her head and she longed for her DVD player and 55" HD TV so she could watch it again. But those days were over. He'd never let her go now, not when he needed her to be his eyes and ears inside the shop.

As the tiny witch flattened herself out on the side of the cup and fell into what passed for sleep, the man on the receiving end of the message, sitting alone in his study as always, watched the pawns arrange themselves. When he was satisfied that they were done, he touched the harp to translate the notes, listening as the instrument's voice sang, "Ding dong the witch is dead." No need to seek a reference for that lyric. The do-gooder Hereditarium were so very kind to do his dirty work for him. Now the next phase of his plan could begin, free of lingering impediments, and this time, he would not fail.

ALSO BY JULIETTE HARPER

This book is the third
in *The Jinx Hamilton Mystery Series.*
The next in the series will be *Witch on First*
coming soon on Amazon.

Witch at Heart - Jinx Hamilton Book 1
Witch at Odds - Jinx Hamilton Book 2

Juliette Harper is also the author of *The Lockwood Legacy.*
Six full-length books are currently available in that series including:

Langston's Daughters
Baxter's Draw
Alice's Portrait
Mandy's Father
Irene's Gift
Jenny's Choice

These books may also be purchased
in two specially priced collections:

The Lockwood Legacy Books 1-3
and
The Lockwood Legacy Books 4-6

The Lockwood Legacy includes

a companion set of short stories.

The first two installments are:

Langston's Ghost: Aftermath

Langston's Ghost: From Limbo to Lust

Other works in Juliette Harper's catalog include

the *Selby Jensen Paranormal Mysteries,*

the *Study Club Mysteries*,

the *Fermata Post-Apocalyptic Series*,

and the *Before Series* of short-story romances.

Selby Jensen Paranormal Mysteries

Descendants of the Rose

The Study Club Mysteries

You Can't Get Blood Out of Shag Carpet

The Before Series

Before Marriage

The Fermata Series

ABOUT THE AUTHOR

Juliette Harper is the pen name used by the writing team of Patricia Pauletti and Rana K. Williamson. As a writer, Juliette's goal is to create strong female characters facing interesting, challenging, painful, and at times comical situations. Refusing to be bound by genre, her primary interest lies in telling good stories.

Six of Juliette's series are currently available. The best-selling *Lockwood Legacy*, is a nine-book chronicle of the lives of three sisters who inherit a ranch in Central Texas following their father's suicide. The first six novels appeared in 2015: *Langston's Daughters, Baxter's Draw, Alice's Portrait, Mandy's Father, Irene's Gift,* and *Jenny's Choice*. The seventh, *Kate's Journey*, will be available later in 2016.

Descendants of the Rose is the first installment of the Selby Jensen Paranormal Mysteries. The second book, *Lost in Room 636*, will also be available in 2016. Selby's business card reads "Private Investigator," but to say the least, that downplays her real occupation where business as usual is anything but normal.

And don't miss the hilariously funny "cozy" *Study Club Mysteries*, a light-hearted spin off of *The Lockwood Legacy*. Set in the 1960s, this series takes on the often-absurd eccentricities of small town life with good-natured, droll humor. The first book, *You Can't Get Blood Out of Shag Carpet*, is already listed in the Amazon store with *You Can't Put a Corpse in a Parade* coming soon.

Juliette has also made forays into the arena of short fiction arena with *Before Marriage*, a light, sweet romance and *Langston's Ghost*, a short-story companion to *The Lockwood Legacy* books.

Fermata: The Winter is the first in a four-novella post-apocalyptic survival series. Five years after an unknown virus divided the world into the living and the dead, four survivors stumble into a winter sanctuary. Brought together by circumstance, but bound by the will to stay alive, a concert pianist and a girl from South Boston forge a friendship and a purpose to cope with their new reality.

Juliette's newest series, *The Jinx Hamilton Mysteries* opens with *Witch at Heart*, a lighter paranormal tale featuring a heroine who possesses powers she never dreamed existed. Jinx has been minding her own business working as a waitress at Tom's Cafe and keeping up with her four cats. Then she inherits her Aunt Fiona's store in neighboring Briar Hollow, North Carolina *and* learns that her aunt has willed her special "powers" to Jinx as well. They say admitting you have a problem is the first step and Jinx has a major problem. She's a new witch and she has no earthly clue what that means — until she's given the opportunity to use her magic to do a good thing.

In Book 2, *Witch at Odds,* Jinx accepts her new life as a witch and is determined to make a success of both that and her new business. However, she has a great deal to learn. As the story unfolds, Jinx sets out to both study her craft and to get a real direction for her aunt's haphazard approach to inventory. Although Jinx can call on Aunt Fiona's ghost for help, the old lady is far too busy living a jet set afterlife to be worried about her niece's learning curve. That sets Jinx up to make a major mistake *and* to figure out how to set things right again.

By Book 3, *Witch at Last*, A lot has changed for Jinx in just a few months. After the mishaps that befell her in *Witch At Odds*, she just wants to enjoy the rest of the summer, but she's not going to be that lucky. As she's poised to tell her friends she's a witch, secrets start popping out all over the place. Between old foes and new locations, Jinx isn't going to get her peaceful summer, but she may just get an entirely different world.

For more information

www.julietteharper.com
julietteharperbooks@gmail.com

By Juliette Harper
Copyright 2016, Juliette Harper

Skye House Publishing

License Notes

ISBN: 978-1-943516-88-9

❀ Created with Vellum

Printed in Great Britain
by Amazon